Sabotaged Christmas

An Appleton, WV Romantic Mystery

Carole Brown

Story and Logic Media Group
Printed in the USA
... For the discriminating reader
...because we believe story *needs* logic.

Sabotaged Christmas: © 2015 by Carole Brown
An Appleton, WV Romantic Mystery

 **Published by STORY AND LOGIC Media
Group, New Carlisle, OH 45344
... For the discriminating reader ...
Because we believe story *needs* logic.**

Cover Design by SAL media
Printed in the USA

ISBN 13: 978-1-941622087
ISBN 10: 1-941622089

Library of Congress Cataloging-in-Publication Data
Brown, Carole
Title: /Carole Brown
ISBN 1-941622089   (paperback)

    1.   Series Fiction 2.   Cozy Mystery 3. Romance.

I. Title. Library of Congress Control Number: 2015954644

Carole Brown

An Appleton, WV Romantic Mystery

The Snowman gave
them a cocky grin.
What did he know?

Sabotaged
Christmas

Dedication:

For all those people who shall remain unnamed, but who have encouraged and prayed for me and my writing attempts, this one's for you.

Praise for Sabotaged Christmas

In **Sabotaged Christmas,** author Carole Brown has constructed a page-turning story with memorable characters and a unique plot with plenty of twists and turns that kept me guessing almost to the end.

Peg Phifer, author
To See the Sun
Somehow Christmas Will Come

Carole Brown has done a wonderful job of balancing romance and mystery, keeping her readers engaged while at the same time entertained. This book is a good read for anyone who loves curling up with a good book, one that will cement your faith in happy endings.

--Barbara Derksen, author of the Wilton/Strait and Finder Keepers Mystery series

Sabotaged Christmas involves sabotage on the work site, romance, and dysfunctional families ... how could that combination result in a warm, fuzzy Christmas ending? Characters I loved and wanted to have their dreams come true. Others, I wanted to keep my distance from and hoped they would get their just deserts. Plot twists I didn't see coming kept me reading past bedtime! I especially liked the ending with all the threads tied together! Well done, Carole.

Carol A. Brown (the other Carol Brown) Author of The Mystery of Spiritual Sensitivity Highly Sensitive and The Sassy Pants Series. Retired Educator.

Carole Brown has done it again in this story. Another down-to-earth rendering that will keep your interest to the very end.

Doubles' Roofing and Siding Company

In **Sabotaged Christmas**, Carole Brown weaves an enticing web of intrigue, romance and faith guaranteed to keep you reading until the very last page. Though set in the dead of winter, this book is sizzling with action, mystery and down-to-earth characters that will keep your imagination spinning and the questions flowing. With its focus on family and the idea of building new relationships, this book is a great example of "love conquers all."

Dana Rongione, author
The Giggles and Grace series
The Delaware Detectives Mystery series

Acknowledgments:

Where would authors be without their critique partners and editors?

Your faithfulness and diligent work toward helping me bring this book to fruition is immeasurable!

Chapter One

Antonietta DeLuca's glance probed the dark shadows in the front yard of the Wisecup job. The streetlight lit up the orange-leafed maple tree, setting it on fire. The tree limbs dipped and swayed to the whispering music from the autumn wind. Fallen leaves crackled to the left of the empty house she faced. Something moved, and Toni shifted to stare at the spot.

With a screech, two cats shot past her and crossed the street, yowling like demons in the night.

Hands shaking, Toni glared at the scattering offenders and leaned against the mailbox, dragging in deep breaths.

She shouldn't have come by herself, but she'd never worried about that before. Her supervisor had begged her to avoid lonely places by herself. Yet she'd needed to do the final inspection of the repairs before signing off on one of their last big projects of the year. With Christmas coming and a long winter ahead, that meant money in her pocket and her employees' pockets.

Drawing in another deep breath, she started up the sidewalk and pulled from her pocket the key to the house. The lock clicked, and a faint, far-off shuffle brushed against her senses.

Head cocked, she listened. Had that sound come from inside the house? Her lips whispered a prayer even as she twisted the knob and gave the door the slightest push. Down the long hallway a light bounced from one of the side rooms.

Bounced? A candle? No, a flashlight.

Someone was in this house.

Reason said to run for help. Tenacity said she couldn't afford to have this job tampered with. Too much effort, too much time, too much money was involved.

Teeth clenched, Toni moved forward and grabbed one of the old umbrellas hanging from a line of hooks. Better than nothing. Her lips wanted to twitch at the ridiculous picture she made, but the fear was too great for levity. Another five feet, and she was at the doorway of the great room.

Someone stood poised at the window, a long and thin object raised. Ready to break the window they faced? A hoodie covered his head, the dark helping to hide his face.

The fear drained away. "Hey. What are you doing?"

The figure whirled, hesitated and ran toward her, the gadget he held pointed at her.

Toni stumbled backward.

The person shoved past, swiped at her shoulder, missed, and fled down the hall.

"Stop." Toni followed, skirted the half-open exterior door, and tripped, sprawling on the concrete porch.

Pain shot through her knee, and she grimaced. Struggling to her feet, she limped down the steps and to the street.

No sign of the intruder. Toni bent and rubbed her knee. But when she straightened, she saw the man, black jacket, hood off his head, at the corner of the street. He seemed to be hesitating as if he'd call out to her, and then he trotted toward her.

Was he the intruder? She studied his clothes, his height and build. But everything had happened too fast. It was impossible to know for sure.

She frowned at him. What was he doing? Coming back for another attack?

Fingers curled into a fist, she marched down the road to meet him. "What do you think you're doing?"

She was close enough now to see a brow lift, the shadows in his eyes questioning her mentality.

"I'm walking home." Said as if wondering why it was her business, and then he probed, "Are you okay?"

He didn't need to think he'd get off that easy. Suspicion reared its head. "Why wouldn't I be?"

His glance dipped to her legs. "Well, you are limping."

"I am. Because of you."

"Me? It's my fault you're limping?" Were his lips twitching?

Too much denial. A sure sign of a lie. "Were you in the house?"

"What house?"

"My house."

"And which house is that?"

Toni shot him a dagger-like look. "Do you live around here?

"Sort of." He shrugged

"What kind of answer is that?"

"One that's vague and thin on information. It's dangerous to be out so late at night by yourself."

Her heart jumped to her throat. Did she dare ask any more questions? Like *why* he'd invaded the house her team had finished remodeling today. "Is that a threat?"

"No. Not at all. Where do you live?"

As if she'd tell him. "I don't know you."

"And I don't know you." He grinned. "I've got to go. Have an early day tomorrow. See you around."

Maybe. She was sure as anything this man was the one in the house. She had no proof. Knew nothing about him. But she would. First thing tomorrow. She'd had enough threats.

~*~

The pink envelope stuck out from the untidy pile of mail Roxie dumped on her desk the next morning. Toni plucked it from the rest.

She stared at the envelope, the elegant handwritten address. No return address, but the postal mark said Appleton. Lifting it to her nose, she sniffed. Her stomach revolted at the cloying wisteria scent. As if handling a live bomb, Toni lifted the flap and withdrew the single flimsy card.

Time's running out. For you. And your dad.

For her dad? That didn't make sense. Toni let go of the missive, and it fluttered to her desktop and laid there, the taunting words daring her to ignore it.

Two weeks ago on a Friday, the first had arrived in all its gaudy glory. She'd laughed and almost tossed the silly card into the trash. At the last minute, she'd stuffed both envelope and card into a side drawer and forgotten about it.

The second arrived the following week. Her heart beat just a bit quicker, but she refused to give in to the panic. Someone playing a prank. Not very clever or even funny. Into the drawer it'd gone with the first.

But the damage on their current construction site had been annoying and scary. Not only in lost labor time, but having to re-stock the stolen material had put a serious damper on her spirits. And the company bank account.

She laid all three notes side by side and studied them.

Leave town on your own or I'll force you!

Everyone knows what a fake your father was.

And now: *Time's running out. For you. And your dad.*

They'd all been handwritten so neatly, so precisely.

Her father? A fake? What kind of sick person thought this was funny? Her father was one of the best, and everyone in Appleton knew it. It was impossible for private matters to be kept quiet in a small town. But she had no secrets, and she'd never given a thought her father might have any.

Besides, it was all nonsense and a lie. Her father would have told her if there'd been secrets.

Wouldn't he?

"To-ni."

Toni snatched the pink intrusions and threw them back into their hiding place as the door to her office opened, and a bush of red hair thrust itself in. A hand lifted and touched the extra-large, sparkling hairclip attempting to hold back the thick strands from the powdered, freckled face. "Are you ready? Rod's here."

"I'm on my way." Toni grabbed her jacket and briefcase.

"Hey, how's our girl doing?" Tall, lanky, fifty-six-year-old Rod Polinsky leaned against the desk where Roxie, the mop-haired redhead, brandished a nail file like a weapon.

"Are you okay?" Roxie arched an overly plucked brow at her, her eyes drilling through the façade of normalness Toni pasted on her face.

She winced. She'd never been much good hiding anything from Roxie's x-ray eyes.

Toni tried. She really did. But nothing would ever convince her secretary and construction supervisor that she had grown up. To them, she was forever stuck in her teen years.

"I'm fine."

"You sure?"

"Why are you asking?" Better to tease her out of her over-concern as to take it seriously.

Roxie resumed her filing, and only glanced at Toni again when she delivered her bombshell. "I overheard Sylvia Searles talking to some of the ladies of the church. Pretty agitated, she was."

"And what does that have to do with me?"

"You were her topic of discussion. Seems you've upset her again by your refusal to attend the annual Christmas banquet at Arnie's place of business."

"Oh, dear. Not again. If only she'd leave poor Arnie alone, he'd find someone soon enough."

"I think the man in question is in love with you." Roxie insisted.

"Nonsense. He only thinks that because his mother won't let him think anything else."

"You can't force love, Roxie. You know that." Rod straightened. "It'll work itself out once Arnie decides to do his own choosing. Don't bug Toni about it."

"I'm just saying." Roxie pouted.

"Enough about that." Toni smiled at Rod. "Ready to get that new contract signed and sealed?"

"Sure am. I promised to give all four of our guys a call tonight. A little pre-Christmas promise they can share with their families."

"Right. Let's go then."

She closed her mind to her unwanted secret mail. All her attention needed to be riveted on getting this contract. No need to focus on what she didn't understand.

~*~

"This is it?" Toni stared at the old fashion house with the broad, wrap-around porch. "That's odd."

"What's the matter, Toni?

"I don't know, but I have a funny feeling. Like I've been here before, but as far as I can remember, I haven't." She shook her head. "I guess its déjà vu kicking in, huh?"

Toni eyed the front of the house. It could have been a handsome place, but let go, it had become the worst on the block, and the lack of any sign of Christmas decorations made it stick out like a swollen stubbed toe.

Definitely in need of construction repairs and some Christmas spirit.

"Could be, but right now, all you need to do is concentrate on getting this contract signed."

"You're right. That's priority. Coming?"

Rod shoved a hand over his head, smoothing back his grayish blond hair in a style reminiscent of the fifties—a blond Elvis. "You can handle it. If you don't mind, I'll sit here and enjoy my music."

Toni chuckled and swung her door open. Rod might come across as an old time rock 'n roller, but he was bluegrass all the way.

A sense of relief washed over her as she knocked on the door. *Wrong* door. She distinctly remembered an oak door, plain, no windows.

She'd never been here.

"*You're* Toni DeLuca?

Toni looked up. The man from last night faced her, and her mouth dropped open. "What are you doing here?"

"I live here."

"You live here? In this house? In Appleton?"

"Is that a problem?" His eyes narrowed. "Why are *you* here?"

Turning the tables, was he? Thinking he could run over her with his questions? "I came to-to..."

There went that left brow. Amused, again? Laughing at her confusion?

"I do have an appointment..." He made a show of glancing at his expensive watch. "...right about now, if you don't have anything better to do than annoy your neighbors. At least, I'm assuming that's what you are."

She opened her mouth to refute his unfair accusation when she saw his mouth twitch. He *was* laughing. At her. Pretending he didn't know why she was here.

He clicked his fingers and pointed at her. "I've got it. You're the secretary at DeLuca Construction. Could you run along and tell your boss—Tony Deluca, was it?—that I prefer to deal with him?'

Was he serious? He was awfully good at avoiding her questions. And making her look like the idiot.

"No, I'm not." She looked up at him standing in the doorway and swallowed. She wanted to badger him into confessing about last night, but with the promise of a much-needed contract, she wouldn't. Toni bit back her sarcasm. "I've brought the contract by for you to sign. *I* own DeLuca Construction."

"I thought..." The man paused, took off his glasses, and rubbed at his eyes. "I thought when I talked previously with the secretary, Toni DeLuca was a man. Is he one of your employees?"

"Rod?"

"No. Toni Deluca."

Were the names bothering the man? Or was he uncomfortable hiring her company because he had an agenda against them? "Rod supervises DeLuca Construction. *I* own the business."

"And you are Toni DeLuca?"

Hadn't she just said so? What was wrong with him?

Toni shifted just enough so she could cast a glance back at Rod sitting at the curb in her 56

Chevy truck, bluegrass Christmas music blasting from a CD. He lifted a hand. His broad, tanned face spread in a you're-my-pal grin. Bushy eyebrows rose as if asking if she needed help.

"So you want to build my addition?" The man in the doorway followed her gaze and seemed to be studying the violet-colored truck. He swung his gaze back to her. His face clouded. "I doubt you could lift a hammer, let alone a board."

Ah, ha. He must have finally figured out who she was.

"Of course I can, but DeLuca construction will build your addition." Toni eyed her prospective client—a client she'd thought she had sewed up and in the bag. Well, this guy wasn't the first prospective client she'd had to reassure to gain the work. She took a deep breath, gripped her clipboard tighter, and eased into her coaxing mode.

"I won't be doing the actual work. Rod..." Toni nodded at the truck with the big man inside it. "...and my four workers will do it. I'm just here with the contract for you. As soon as this is signed, I'll be out of your hair—so to speak. We'll be able to start, and the sooner we start, the sooner the job will be finished."

Toni flapped a sheaf of papers, and Perrin's gaze took in her gesture. As far as she could tell, her words made not the slightest impression on him. "I think I've a good idea of what you want regarding the addition. Rod and I went over your plans pretty thoroughly, and I made it a priority to get the contract right for you. Anyone in town can vouch for the DeLuca

Company—and me."

Maybe it would have been better for Roxie to never have gotten the phone call from Mr. Douglas two months ago when he'd inquired about hiring them. Lord knew, since she'd inherited her dad's business, she'd had her share of disgruntled clients wanting unrealistic results.

The promise of this job meant a lot to her men. Rod and Roxie, and the four laborers depended on DeLuca Construction for their livelihood. On her. Right now, filling that need meant getting this job.

Toni shivered in the blast of cold air and glanced again at Rod. He grinned, shrugged, and nodded his head. Meaning, rein in her temper and get the job.

Douglas grimaced and stepped back. "Well, in spite of your nosiness and a little bit of weirdness last night, I know I don't have time to research and locate another company. Come in, and we'll talk."

Toni clamped her mouth shut to keep from spewing out words she knew she'd regret, and stepped inside. Her gaze fastened on the long walking stick leaning in the corner of the hallway. The weapon he'd tried to use last night to break her shoulder?

Her gaze flickered back to his face.

Chapter Two

"I take it Perrin Douglas gave you some trouble." Rod stretched his long legs.

"He seemed to think I wasn't big or strong enough to get the job done."

Rod guffawed. "Did you tell him you cut your teeth on a two by four?"

"He finally—reluctantly, I'm sure—admitted he wanted us to do the job." Toni nodded at the contract. "It's all signed and dated."

"Great. He agreed to the remodeling and the addition?"

"Yes."

The grin splitting her supervisor's face was answer enough. He was pleased.

Toni backed into the street, but glanced at the house. Perrin stood at the window watching them. For a minute she thought he would wave. Instead, he turned and disappeared.

Childishly, she geared down the truck and left a short strip of rubber. So much for appearing mature and capable. If her newest client heard that, it would only serve to justify his initial judgment of her.

"Feeling a mite frustrated at someone?"

Rod's dry question plucked her spirits from the floor of the truck, and she gave him a look. "Yeah, I guess I was. Sorry. I'll behave."

He said nothing more only allowed his eyes

to twinkle at her. Thankfully, he understood what aggravation clients could be.

Toni wheeled into DeLuca's parking lot, and they hopped out. Shoving open the office door, Rod waited for Toni to enter before heading straight for the receptionist desk. He bent over to swipe a kiss onto Roxie's cheek.

"When you two get done smooching, mind if we have a short meeting?" Toni grinned at them.

Rod straightened and winked at his wife. "Got any coffee? Sounds as if the boss means business."

~*~

Perrin wended his way through the maze of cardboard boxes still left to unpack.

What a nuisance. This should have been done weeks ago. On a deadline and two weeks behind in his writing, there had not been enough time. Maybe he could hire someone to do the rest of the unpacking, but that would mean noise and people about. He didn't need any more distractions.

Why couldn't life be simple? And now he'd gone and hired a woman construction boss who'd clutter up his life even more.

Women were too temperamental. Experience had taught him that. Not one thing he and Marge ever tried to do, but what it had to be her way. Changing their plans two or three times was a normal routine for his wife.

Tell a man what you wanted, and you got it. Tell a woman, and she'd try to talk you out of it every time. Always thought there was a better way.

Marge's eternal parade of comments

battered at his mind. But he wouldn't go there today. Her actions while alive, and her death—he couldn't think about them now. He had to get back to his writing.

Perrin measured coffee grounds and then plugged in the coffeemaker. Drumming his fingers on the countertop, he watched the drip-after-drip and wished the coffee would flow faster.

That DeLuca girl—well, woman, he supposed—didn't look any older than eighteen. How could anyone so petite run a construction business? Weren't those businesses kind of...rough? The men hard to handle? Maybe she had women working for her. A female construction crew.

No, she'd definitely said she had four guys working for her. He'd been alert enough to catch that.

He dug into a box for his favorite stoneware mug and then poured a cup of the dark rich brew he loved and took a sip.

The door banged open. "Dad."

"What?" His hand jerked and the hot, hot coffee splashed onto his fingers. Now he was snapping at his son. Perrin softened his voice. "What is it, Blake?"

Blake headed for the refrigerator. He poured a tall glass of milk and slumped into a chair. "I like Miss DeLuca."

Perrin didn't bother asking how his son could possibly know her enough to like or dislike. Or how he'd met her.

He studied his long-legged son and smiled. "So you liked her?"

"Yep. I mean, yes. Running a construction

business? How cool is that?" Blake slanted his eyes toward him.

Perrin had not been impressed with her or her business, which was probably unfair. Her huge dark eyes, sparkling with gold flecks, had drawn him like a magnet as much as he didn't want to admit it. But he also knew what a gullible person he was.

The lump in his throat expanded. His wife's eyes had captivated him as well, and look where that had gotten him. He stiffened his resolve and snapped his attention back to his son. "She could be a very poor manager. What woman knows much about carpentry?"

"You don't know *her*."

The hair on Perrin's arms stood up. Blake sounded just like his mother who used to ridicule Perrin on everything. Her musical laughing voice had reined him in, but later that same voice belittled most of his comments. Jaw clenched, he said, feeling like he was explaining, "Well, I signed the contract."

"Sid says his dad hired DeLuca's to do a pretty big job for them, and they did great. Sid's dad says they're the best construction business around." Blake took a long gulp of his milk, and then stuffed a chocolate chip cookie into his mouth.

Perrin looked at his son in astonishment. "Why on earth did Sid tell you all that?"

A bony shoulder lifted. "I asked him if he knew anything about them when you were going over the bids."

The two families probably went to the same church. Or were in a club of some sort. Or whatever. Didn't small town people know everyone else? Naturally they'd vouch for each other.

No need to try to change his son's mind. Blake had decided to champion Toni DeLuca, and nothing would stop him. "Women do most anything they want nowadays. I don't fault them for it. I just hope I did the right thing hiring her business. And I hope she has enough sense to leave the work up to her men."

"Give her a chance."

Perrin gave his son a sharp glance. That was a tinge of mockery in the kid's voice. He was a good boy, but much too precocious for his age.

Marge's husky voice echoed in his mind.

I'm going to have it the way I want or not at all.

And she had. Right up to the day of her death.

~*~

Perrin's mind refused to let go of the memories that tore through him and left him a shred of his former self.

He should have recognized his wife's usual taunts for what they were. Meaningless threats. He should have ignored them and forgiven her. Instead, he'd fired back the words that sent her out the door in a fit of uncontrollable rage—and her death.

The doorbell chimed.

Perrin stared at the door, hating to answer, hoping it wasn't the construction owner knocking at his door again, forcing the haunting memories to resurface. Reluctantly, he opened the door and stared at the two women standing on his porch.

"Hi, I'm Rita Mae Simpson and the chairperson of Appleton's Welcoming Committee. I wanted to personally welcome you to our town."

"I'm Sylvia Searles, your neighbor." The second woman, a trim blond that looked her age and dressed ten years younger, held out a luscious-looking pie. "Apple pie for the new man on the block."

Before Perrin could accept the gift, Rita Mae thrust a cloth covered basket at him. "I hope you like homemade bread and locally-made apple cider. I also put in some samples of my café's specialty coffee. You do drink coffee?"

She peered up at him, her eyes bright with a teasing light, her lips curved in a solicitous smile.

"Thanks. I'm afraid I'll have to admit I'm a coffee addict." He tossed a glance at the blond. "And an apple pie lover."

"Then you'll enjoy *my* homemade apple pie with that coffee." Sylvia beamed at him.

"Straight from the nearest bakery, Perrin. Don't be fooled. Sylvia can't bake canned biscuits." Rita Mae's laugh was a mixture of flirtatious fun and shrill edginess. "May I come in?"

The mountain of work needing finished leaped to the forefront of his thoughts, but he grimaced—inside—and stepped back.

Rita Mae strolled toward the kitchen, peering in rooms as she went almost as if she knew the place well.

"Still the same as ever."

"How would you know?" Sylvia's eyes had

narrowed in suspicion.

The dark brunette swished away from the blond. "Just because we're friends doesn't mean you know everything about me, Sylvia. Really? You're showing your ignorance. Again."

The other woman's face flushed. Anger sparks flashed then died in her eyes. She edged closer to Perrin and smiled.

But Perrin ignored their obvious flirting with him and their bickering with each other, and focused on Rita Mae's observation of his home. He was guessing she'd been inside here. And why not? Whoever owned it before probably were friends of hers. "Friends owned this place?"

"Family. My uncle and aunt, years ago. When they moved to Charleston, it stood empty. Now that they're gone, the executor of the will put it on the market. I've been dying to know what you've done to it."

"Nothing yet. I've hired DeLuca's Construction to build an addition."

The look she cast at him was definitely filled with curiosity. His simple comment had aroused an alertness in her.

"Oh. Really?" Her question begged for a response from him.

"What do you mean?"

"I don't like to spread tales..."

He leaned forward. "Then why tell me? It's not like you know me."

"Normally I wouldn't." She simpered and nudged his shoulder with hers.

The inelegant snort from the blond would have ordinarily given him a laugh. Their fussing was either from a may-the-best-woman-win competitive variety or pure jealousy. He didn't have time to figure it out.

"If it's something I need to hear, please tell me."

"Lately, Toni's been acting strange."

"As in?"

"I don't know you. Perhaps I shouldn't say anything."

"Aren't you the welcoming committee chairperson? Shouldn't you warn me about companies not on the up and up?"

"You're right." She eyed him as if deciding how much to share. "Toni's been having some trouble lately with her construction jobs. Material missing, delays in starting and finishing the jobs. Things like that."

Perrin raised a brow as the only answer he was willing to give right now.

I heard…" Blondie hurried to add her opinion. "…she's stealing her own material for insurance reasons. I know she put in a recent insurance claim."

"Is that right?"

Blondie nodded, her lips pursed in a shy-like smile.

"You can do as you please. Just be careful." Rita Mae moved closer and smiled up into his eyes.

"I will." He wanted to groan aloud. What had he gotten himself into? "Tell me, what's Appleton like?"

"Lovely, old town. Pure West Virginia. Close knit, but friendly."

She moved toward the door, and Perrin followed, hoping they'd both decide to leave together.

"Well, I must run. Stop by anytime at the shop, and if you need anything, *call me*."

She laid a manicured hand on his arm, batted her eyelashes, and Perrin forced back the reaction to pull away. He wasn't at all sure he'd ask any woman for help, but it was a friendly gesture for her to make. No need to be rude. He lifted the basket. "I appreciate this. We'll enjoy the contents."

She walked down the sidewalk and wiggled her fingers at him before opening her car door.

He tensed as she paused, afraid she would head back to his door.

Instead she called. "Don't forget now. I'm looking forward to showing you our sights."

He and Sylvia watched the car spin out of the driveway and down the road. When he glanced at the blond, her expression told him not all was roses and cream in their friendship.

"So you two are friends?"

The woman cast him a glance. "Yeah. Sometimes."

"Isn't Toni DeLuca in your circle of friends?"

"Now that's a question that begs to be answered." She stepped off the porch and gave him a finger wave, an accurate imitation of Rita Mae's.

~*~

Inside her office Toni waited on Rod and Roxie to join her. She stood in front of her desk. Mr. Douglas had been decent enough once he had gotten over his twenty-questions phase. But his troubled eyes haunted her. She didn't want to admit it, given his actions last night.

She sighed. Thank God, she'd arrived in

time to prevent another sabotaged job. It was heartbreaking to near the end of an expensive job and have it destroyed. She'd barely been able to recover from all the loss from that previous job.

Although her business insurance company promised a hefty check, she'd yet to see it.

Toni slid a hand over the smooth finish of the cherry desk she claimed for her own. She loved the feel of finished wood. Her heart warmed as she admired the grain of the dark stained wood. Still as gorgeous as when her dad had used it.

The memory of her father lifting Toni in the air, his handsome face lined in a broad smile, swirled through her mind. She'd been five. Maybe six. She dug further back into the recesses of her mind. What could she remember before that? Anything? Nothing? She looked down again at her desk and didn't know whether to laugh or cry.

Her father's hand covering her childish one as she learned how to hammer a nail.

His strong arms surrounding her as she climbed her first ladder.

Their laughter as they used rollers and brushes, smudges of paint decorating their faces.

So much to remember from her childhood. Granted, she had few memories of her mother. But so many others.

Toni lifted her head to study the big portrait of her dad she'd hung on the wall across from her desk. Slight and dark as she, Danny Deluca smiled down at her, and his deep brown eyes sent continual messages of love and encouragement.

She blew a kiss his way. "I love you, Daddy."

The office door banged open, and Roxie stuck her head in. Concern deepened the twang in her voice. "You talking to someone?"

"Daddy."

Roxie rolled her expressive eyes and frowned. "We'll be right in. Rod's on the phone."

Toni nodded, but her mind wasn't on her office manager or supervisor.

Her gaze flicked to the drawer hiding the missives. Did someone know something she didn't? Who hated her enough to do something like this? Who was sabotaging her business? And most of all, why? Her mind flipped through all the names of people in Appleton she could think of and discarded one after another.

Chapter Three

That evening Toni dropped her briefcase on the hall table, hung her blue hoodie in the closet, and kicked off her shoes. She hopped first on one foot, then the other, stripping off her socks. Barefooted, she walked to the kitchen.

She needed something to make her forget those pink envelopes with what she hoped were false messages. The salad she'd chopped this morning, waiting in her fridge, held no appeal this evening. Something warm and soothing would ease the hurt in her heart.

Soup.

Homemade wild rice chicken soup would do the trick, and Toni dumped it into a pot. While the soup heated, she lit the logs in the fireplace.

"Hey, Charms, how's your day been?" She knelt to stroke the calico that wound its body around her ankles. "Hungry?"

Chicken-flavored cat food would match her own dinner and maybe keep her cat from begging for hers. Charms stared with yellow-green eyes at her owner and yowled as Toni opened the can.

"Letting me know you're on the verge of starvation, are you?"

She stood at her kitchen window and stroked the cat with her toes. Her gaze took in the neat back yard, the brown dirt of the vegetable garden where she'd harvested tomatoes and green beans and cucumbers. The colorful, veggie-filled jars lined her pantry giving her a happy feeling every time she visited.

Too bad all these good memories couldn't blot out the thought of the notes. Her stomach churned every time she passed them spread out on her island counter.

Was there something in her background Daddy hadn't told her? As far as she knew, she had no enemies. Had her father kidnapped her? She winced. She'd have to have an awful lot of proof before believing that.

Why else drag her into these accusations if she wasn't involved?

Had he been a criminal hiding from big city law? Had he committed fraud somewhere before her time? Stolen identities or concocted some huge scam?

Toni poured the soup in a large mug, her own garden-grown spices drifting upward to tingle her nose. She arranged wheat crackers, several thin slices of pepper jack cheese, and a tart Granny Smith apple on a plate.

As she passed her alcove window, she set down the tray and snipped off a sprig of peppermint from her winter collection of herbs in their orange clay pots. Then she carried the food on her best tray to the living room, settled on a rug and leaned back against the stone hearth.

She lifted the mint, closed her eyes and sniffed, hoping the scent would overwhelm the words in those small messages that haunted her.

She would have to do some probing, but that meant asking questions and digging into places she might wish she'd never stuck a spade into. She wasn't sure she was ready to deal with everyone in Appleton speculating on her and her life. But to get answers? She had no choice.

She couldn't live with this constant hassle and doubt.

Toni spooned her soup steadily. With the last bite, she shoved aside the mug and rested her head against the stone of the fireplace, the warmth seeping into her skin.

Eyes closed, she pictured her father's black hair, his smiling brown eyes, his suave attitude. She didn't need anyone to tell her how much she resembled the man she'd always called dad. But did she really? Was it a coincidence that she looked like the man who raised her?

No man had ever quite compared to him in her childish eyes. The only parent she could remember.

Wouldn't her father have told her if something was wrong? She couldn't remember a time when he didn't take her to church. He'd been a steady, good influence on her. He wouldn't have lied to her. Not her father.

Toni moved restlessly. She was making way too much of those cards. Someone was playing a very stupid trick. She needed to concentrate on somehow preventing anymore vandalism.

The firecracker bang on her front door sent her heart leaping higher than the house she called home.

~*~

Perrin stared at the contract he'd signed that afternoon then removed his glasses and wished he'd done more checking. That welcoming woman's casual warning had sent his antenna weaving. This was a big undertaking. The first since his wife's death. If he'd had his mind on it instead of bemoaning what couldn't be changed, this might not have happened. "I should have asked around."

With his long legs flung over the arm of a chair, Blake looked up from his book. "What?"

"Talking to myself, son. Nothing you'd be interested in." Perrin scattered the papers.

"I might. Tell me."

Perrin leveled a look at his son. He wouldn't put it pass the boy to understand better than he himself did. "I'm not sure I made the right decision in choosing the DeLuca's. Miss Simpson let me know there's been some dissatisfaction with her work."

"That woman. I didn't like her."

Obviously, he'd been in the background listening to the welcoming lady's comments.

"I like Miss Deluca."

Easy enough for a kid to say. His son never met a stranger, while he'd always been a loner, a geek in a literary world. A person who could write his thoughts but struggled to voice them in a social realm.

Blake tilted his head, his eyes scrunched up. "Go talk with her."

Leave it to a kid to get right down to the nitty-gritty of a problem. What Blake said made sense, and there was no reason not to discuss his concerns with Miss DeLuca. He'd hired her firm. She was working for him. "You're right."

"I know I am." The boy slouched back on the sofa beside his father, his tone bossy and a little bit know-it-all. "Haven't you always taught me to think for myself and then make decisions? That's what I've done with Toni DeLuca."

His son's tone and voice was an echo from Marge's mouth.

After Marge's death, he'd vowed never to trust another woman. But this morning—when he'd seen the DeLuca woman on his porch, he'd trusted her instinctively. Regardless of last night's strange confrontation when he'd been out walking. Or that he didn't want to. Those clear eyes. Her bubbling personality. The sincerity radiating from her. All of it encouraged trust.

He'd been mistaken about Marge. Had thought her the real thing when he'd married her, and if he could be mistaken then, why not now?

He wanted to believe the DeLuca woman could be trusted to tell him the truth, to handle his job with professionalism, to get the work done. But his gut told him not to walk into the same trap twice.

~*~

According to his visitor this morning—the brunette—this town was idyllic. His gaze took in the peaceful community as he drove, the houses in the modest to pricey range, and all the neat lawns. Just the place to finish his work.

And get away from everyone who knew him.

It was good for his son too. He hadn't realized how confining his work at the college had been for his son until they'd moved here. Away from the busy life his father led and past memories, Blake had expanded into a person in his own right. A twelve-year-old-going-on-fifteen.

Lined with ancient oaks and maples, the houses were small but well kept. Perrin slowed and read the house numbers. One tall, distinguished-looking man in a long overcoat, turned as he passed and lifted a hand in greeting. The town was certainly friendly. More so than the big town he'd come from.

The scrolled seventeen shone in the porch light. The quiet street was empty of strollers except for a lone figure half-trotting down the street as if late for an appointment. He'd almost passed when he gave the person a double-take.

Was that the woman who'd welcomed him earlier? Rita Mae something-or-the-other? Maybe, but that meant nothing. She could be Toni DeLuca's neighbor for all he knew.

After pulling into Miss DeLuca's driveway, he sat in his car and looked at her home. The place resembled a large cottage, the outside tastefully decorated with colored lights, the porch simply decorated with package-filled baskets and a single tree topped with a bright star.

As nervous as a young person seeking their first job, Perrin stared at his reflection in the rearview mirror. He'd changed into khakis and a casual tan and rust striped shirt. His dark sweater pulled the outfit together. Not too bad.

Casual but dressy enough for business.

He hated confrontations. Had enough of them to last several life times. He hated even worse being tricked. If this meeting had to be done, there was no use putting it off.

Opening the door, he stepped out of his jeep-that-needed-to-be-retired-but-he-refused-to-give-up, and approached the house. He had to step over the fist-sized rock lying halfway from the steps to the door. Raising his hand he started to knock when the door was flung open.

Miss DeLuca stood before him, those gold flecks swimming in her wide-open, dark eyes. Frightened? He actually felt his heart softening.

"You're pounding on my door?"

"What? I just got here." Was she accusing him of something else? He shifted, his heart hardening again. Why did this woman make him feel so gauche? "I had a few questions."

Her gaze wandered to the rock lying on her porch, and if they could, her eyes widened even more.

His own gaze followed hers, and he frowned. "What's this? A new way to trip up those not welcome?"

A quick smile flittered across her face before she sobered. "No, and I'm not using it to decorate. I think someone tossed it at my door." Her lovely eyes were back to questioning him, a touch of suspicion edging her pupils.

Ignoring her attitude, he squatted and studied her door. "Look here, Miss DeLuca."

A second later she knelt beside him.

He raked a finger across a short scratch on

the stained wooden door. "Looks fresh to me."

Her finger shot forward, rested on the door beside his, and traced the scratch.

When she didn't ask the obvious question, he did. "Why? Why would anyone throw a rock at your door?"

She didn't answer, so he went on. "Probably kids, don't you think?"

Her bottom lip trembled.

The unexpected protective urge to shield her swamped him.

She jumped to her feet. "What was it you wanted? You have questions?"

"Yes, if you don't mind?"

Perrin caught the surreptitious glance she gave her wristwatch, then, immediately, she stepped back, an invitation for him to enter.

Odd. What had that reluctance been about? "Thanks."

Perrin followed her as she led the way to her sitting room and motioned for him to take a seat. She chose one of the flowered-patterned wing chairs pulled close to the fireplace, and he sat on the loveseat opposite her.

When she didn't speak, he wanted to frown. Instead, he swallowed his annoyance and looked around the room. "Beautiful fireplace. Did you...?"

"No, my dad built the house for a young couple who soon outgrew it. I always loved the place, and when daddy passed away, I bought it." She gave the fireplace and the mantle above it, filled with her collection of dark objects, a loving look. "I love the cold seasons just so I can use it."

"It feels good tonight. The air has a chill to it

that warns of snow." Perrin shifted in his seat and breathed in the scent of spices and chicken. What on earth was she cooking anyway? The smell was enough to drive any man wild.

His stomach growled. Those two pieces of pizza he'd eaten earlier this evening hadn't done much to satisfy his hunger. But then pizza wasn't his favorite meal.

"Would you like something to drink? Coffee, tea, juice, water?"

He shouldn't, knowing what he'd come for, but he couldn't resist. "No bother for you?" At the shake of her head, he added. "Coffee, then."

She rose, and whirled from the room, calling back over her shoulder. "I'll be just a minute. Why don't you enjoy the fire?"

Perrin rested his head against the back of his chair and contemplated his personal demons as he stared into the blaze of the burning wood.

~*~

Toni left the sitting room, the traitorous bottom lip between her teeth, ashamed Mr. Douglas's somewhat sympathetic attitude had touched her. Spilling her feelings to anyone and everyone had never been her habit. Her father raised her to be independent and confident in her own judgments, and by nature, a friendly and happy person.

Dealing with the two destructive rampages on finished DeLuca remodeling jobs and all the jarring notes to her own person had shaken her. Badly.

Toni placed both hands on the countertop

and growled at herself. *Stop it. Sobbing on an acquaintance—a business customer's shoulder, of all things, is not permitted.* At least not by her. She'd handled the problems so far. She'd continue to do so.

Besides, it was awfully suspicious the man sitting in her living room had shown up last night *and* tonight. Who was to know but he was the culprit? In her eyes—

From outside the window, something moved, and Toni frowned. Charms? No, she seldom allowed her cat outdoor time. A neighbor cat that had strayed into her yard?

The next second, Toni rejected the suggestion as a tall figure scurried from around her building and disappeared. Was that Kevin Myers, her newest employee? Had he wanted to speak with her? Then why the furtive movements?

She watched for a second, almost tempted to run outside and check on her property, but even from here, the light revealed that the garage and exterior walk through doors were intact and still locked.

Toni broke off her thoughts and instructed herself. *Concentrate. Deal with Douglas and his questions tonight.* Tomorrow, she'd begin some research. And find an answer to the ludicrous, but vague, accusations and threats those notes spouted.

She added cream and sugar to the tray and arranged a half dozen homemade, apple-flavored, sugar cookies on a small plate, tucked a paper napkin under the spoon, and reached for a heavy stoneware mug. She poured the dark brew into a matching pitcher, then started to pick up the tray.

Her phone rang, and Toni debated answering it. Whoever it was would call back if it was important. Then she reached for it and spoke. "Toni here."

"Really? You couldn't even help him out for one evening?" Sylvia Searles shrill voice blared into her ear.

Not now. Toni sighed. The woman was determined to throw her son, Arnie Searles, at her.

A year older than Tony, the young man had always jumped when she called, from high school till the present. Rod needed extra help on a particular time-crucial job? Toni rang for Arnie, and he would have personal days he'd use to come to her rescue. A business dinner where she needed an escort? Arnie fit the bill.

But she couldn't, not in the past, and definitely not now, consider him anything but a friend. Her dad had never said a word against him, had liked him, in fact, but Toni had read his unspoken opinion of Arnie and agreed.

He wasn't for her.

"How many times has he come to your rescue when you needed *him*?" Sylvia's tone was a little bit pettish and the question right on the nose.

Still, when he'd invited her last week to a fancy evening for his work, she'd been knee deep in designing Perrin Douglas's addition and had refused.

"I explained to him why I couldn't accept his invitation, Sylvia. Everyone loves him. He's sure to get someone less busy than myself."

Wouldn't do a bit of good to explain. Sylvia had, years ago, set her—Arnie's cap—for Toni, and there was no dissuading her.

"I have company, Sylvia. Have to go." Toni hung up before the woman could throw the obvious question at her, 'Who?'

Toni drew in a breath and closed her eyes. For a half second, guilt stung her. Arnie was a wonderful man, and if Sylvia would back away, make some woman a good husband. Just not her.

Retrieving the tray, she headed back to her guest.

Was Perrin Douglas guilty of sabotaging her business projects? She thought so. He was a man filled with a controversial bundle of emotions, it seemed. A situation that filled her with doubt about her judgment in taking on his job.

Toni didn't often have to show someone how tough she could be, but Danny DeLuca hadn't raised her to take over his business for nothing. If Douglas was attempting to fool her, playing her along while he fulfilled his secret agenda, then she'd suffer through enough of it to find out what. She straightened her shoulders. She was about to put on a display of real toughness.

For an audience of one—Perrin Douglas.

Chapter Four

Toni entered her sitting room and stopped. Mr. Douglas's head lay against the back of her white and burgundy striped loveseat. He appeared to be asleep.

She studied him, her eyes narrowed. Had he come to cancel the contract already? Complain and make changes before they'd even started?

He was a good-looking man, and unfortunately for her, interesting.

Toni pressed her lips together at her softening heart and walked to the coffee table to set the tray down, clattering a little.

The man's eyes popped opened. "Sorry. I must have dozed off."

"Cream, sugar?" Toni leaned forward and poured the mug full of the steaming liquid. At the shake of his head, she added, "Why haven't I seen you around town?"

He took the mug from her, sipped, and lifted it toward her. "Good coffee. Moved here two weeks ago. Hoped I'd have repairs done before then, but understood your company couldn't get it scheduled in then."

What did that mean? Was he complaining? "That's right."

He took another sip of his coffee, but his eyes gazed at her. He reached for a cookie, took a bite, swallowed. "These are good. Did you make them?"

"Yes."

No need to make the conversation too easy for him. If he had a reason for showing up on her doorstep, he'd have to broach the topic. She wouldn't be too eager and give him that satisfaction.

He popped the last third of his cookie in his mouth and eyed the platter, then indicated the room with a broad gesture of his hand. "Beautiful place. Your friends probably beg for invitations."

She couldn't help it. Toni laughed and thought of her two best friends, Starli Cameron and Caroline Gibson. Starli's home was stark to the max. Her Christmas decorations were so simple, yet classy and expensive, one could walk into her house and not realize Christmas was in the air. Caro's apartment was filled with a haber-dash of antiques, used furniture, and dust bunnies. Her decorations—when she remembered to decorate—were a mix and match collection of whatever happened to catch her attention each season. "When they have the time."

"It's hard to imagine a woman liking your type of work."

Toni moved to the fireplace and eyed the man sitting here in her home. "Why?"

He returned her look. "I know absolutely nothing about carpentry. It just seems like a rough type of career."

For a woman. He didn't say the words but he meant them.

Toni stiffened. "Rough? Do you mean hard?"

"That. Aren't the men...?"

"Rod, my supervisor is a Christian and a

gentleman. Two of the other four men who work for DeLuca's Construction are, too."

One of his eyebrows rose. "Meaning?"

"Meaning, the men are respectful to me. They're not angels. Just decent, hard-working men trying to make a living for themselves and their families."

A sudden sheepish expression flit across his face.

Toni couldn't resist the temptation to tease. "You don't do your own minor home repairs?"

The blank expression that covered Perrin Douglas's face fired her desire. "You know, change light bulbs. Put in new faucets. Repair broken windows."

The man shook his head. "We lived on the university grounds. I didn't have the time to worry about those kinds of things."

How could any man not know how to do the basic things around a house? She laughed. "Sorry. You do know how to change a light bulb, right?"

Perrin's face reddened. "Funny, is it? I suppose it is strange. I was wrapped up for years in school, then teaching. Anything we needed done, we hired either the college maintenance man or a recommended guy from the outside. I've never had an interest in...that type of work. And, yes, I can at least change a light bulb."

She shouldn't have teased him. He couldn't help it if he was ignorant. Her lips twitched. He wouldn't appreciate her thinking that. "I'm sorry. The men I was raised around did all their own minor repairs. They only called in the construction companies for something major they didn't want to tackle themselves."

"Still. Why would you like construction work? You don't seem, uh, like the type."

"And what type is that? My dad raised me to take over someday." The tiniest smidgen of irritation rippled through her. "I look at construction as a type of art. I like it even though I don't usually do the actual manual labor any more. But I enjoy pitching in occasionally."

"I see."

"Do you? Let me help you understand my love of construction. Look. See the beauty of the stone? It's called Cherry Log and goes along with the simplicity of this home."

She motioned to him. "Come with me."

Toni led him toward her staircase. "Run your hand over the oak rail. Feel the satiny smoothness. Look at the grain. Isn't it beautiful?"

She moved to the doorway with Perrin following her. She pointed. "Focus in on the room as a whole. See the dark stones blending with the woodwork and how the light colors in the area rugs and furniture tie it all together?"

The tall man beside her took in the room, his gaze roaming about the room.

At last he murmured, grudgingly, but sincere, "A work of love and art."

She nodded, satisfied of his understanding, a twinge of pleasure warming her heart. "Yes. Let's go look at one more thing." She beckoned, and he was on her heels as she went out the back door.

There was no sign of the earlier intruder, yet Toni cast a glance around at her property, just in case.

Her huge garage sat to the left, and back, of her house. She took a key from her pocket, unlocked the side door, and flipped on the overhead light. Inside she gestured at the different piles of wood. "Look at this rough pile of lumber. Then over here's where I've begun the sanding process. See the difference?"

She glided over to where several more were stacked on a pallet and flung out a hand. "Ta Da. The finished product, after repeated sanding, staining, and polyurethane."

Perrin bent over and examined the wood boards. "You did these all by yourself? Looks like a lot of work when you could go buy them ready made."

"You're right, but I'd have to say my finished materials are of a better quality, which gives me satisfaction. More to the point, it's also a relaxing hobby. I don't do a lot of projects from square one, but occasionally, I like to begin from the beginning. Usually something special, and many times I pass it on to someone else."

"What are you building now?" Interest flared in his eyes.

She leaned closer to him and whispered. "Can you keep a secret?"

He stared at her for a moment. "Maybe."

"I'm making a chest to fit under my dining room window, if someone doesn't see it and want it. Hence the secrecy."

"What if I decide *I* want it?"

The unexpected teasing in his voice sent her blood racing.

Toni struck a pose of dismay and wrinkled her nose. "Oh, wow. You wouldn't do that, would you? Seriously, I'd sell it to you, for a pretty penny, mind you."

Perrin laughed. "You're greedy."

Toni smiled up into his eyes. "Yes, I am."

The reminder of who he was and the question of why he'd come battered at her memory. At least, it brought her out of her ever-softening attitude toward him.

"You have this huge building just for building projects?"

Toni locked the door. "No. I also restore cars in the second half of it."

"I can't believe what I'm hearing."

His skepticism sent her ire skyward again. Did he think she was some kind of freak?

Before she could answer, he spoke again, "Don't tell me. Your father taught you that skill too."

"Mostly Rod. I'd hang over his shoulder as he worked, fascinated by the recreation of the cars and probably drove him crazy with all the questions I batted at him. Eventually he gave me one old rusted tin can-of-a-car, and, that, sir, was the beginning of a new love for me." She relaxed and nodded. "I like the older cars, but sell most of them to gain the money to save for what I really want. Someday."

"And what is that?"

Her eyes sparkled with enthusiasm. "Probably a Bentley."

They returned to the house, Toni glanced at her wristwatch, and Perrin followed suit with his own.

He shook his head. "I forgot about my questions. Is it too late to talk about them?"

"Why not stop by the office in the morning,

and we'll talk then?"

He hesitated, but Toni gave him no choice. She smiled at him as she led him to the door. As much as she always tried to please her customers, it was late, and she had an early morning with lots on her plate. It wouldn't hurt Perrin Douglas to wait till tomorrow.

But before she could close the door, he turned back to her. "I saw someone running down the street as I entered your driveway."

"And?"

"Someone threw that rock. Maybe, the person running away?" Perrin gave a nod toward the rock still lying on the porch.

Toni's gaze searched his eyes, looking for she didn't know what, then dropped to the rock lying on her porch. Could it have been Kevin?

Chapter Five

Roxie's cheery face greeted her when Toni shoved through the glass door. Her red hair fanned around her face in a bright flaming halo. "Morning, Toni."

"Phone calls?"

"The messages are on your desk." Roxie dug into a cardboard box and pulled out a one-armed angel with a torn dress, and some scraggly-looking Christmas tree rope. "'Fraid this box is going to have to be tossed."

"Go shopping this afternoon for more. We're the only business on this block without decorations. Better get moving." Toni nodded and headed for her office then turned back before she lost her nerve. She faced the woman who'd been like a mother to her for so many years. "Roxie."

Roxie looked up, her eyes alert, her hands filled with broken ornaments.

"Did you know my mother?"

Roxie shook her head. "You were ten when your dad hired Rod. A short time later I started as his secretary."

Toni frowned. Why hadn't she asked more questions of her father? Why hadn't he told her more? "But you've lived here all your life. Did you ever meet her before you started working for Daddy?"

Roxie's mouth twisted in a wry expression.

"I worked as a cocktail waitress, Toni. That was before Rod and I started to church. It was hardly the same circle your mom and dad traveled in."

Toni wanted to argue. Daddy hadn't a stuck up bone in his body. He never saw a stranger. He was an open, friendly guy with no secrets to hide from anyone.

Or did he?

"What's bothering you?"

Toni let her gaze meet Roxie's. Should she share what those horrid notes said? No. Not yet. If it was someone playing a mean trick, she didn't want people talking. If it were true, she'd tell Roxie soon enough. But maybe one question wouldn't hurt. "But you did know Daddy, right?"

"Yes, but Rod knew him better and longer than I did. I think they worked together before your dad began his own business, when Rod joined him as his supervisor. Why?"

Avoiding Roxie's sharp gaze, Toni entered her office and shut the door. She pushed away the mail Roxie had piled on her desk and glanced at her watch. She would meet with Perrin this morning. At one she had a couple of jobs to check on. Plenty of time to do some research. She'd look for any information she could find about her parents, then on to Perrin Douglas. And maybe have Detective Eddie Snider check out Kevin, her employee. First things first.

When Eddie answered in his lazy, drawn-out voice that sounded as if he'd just awakened from a long nap, she asked, "Can you do me a favor?"

"Hmmm? What's that?"

"Kevin Meyers. Can you do a little background checking on him for me?"

"That your newest employee?"

"Uh, huh."

"Now, Miss Toni. I've known you long enough to know you don't ask for favors unless it's important. Wanna share why you need this?"

Toni hesitated. "Can I take a rain-check? I promise to tell all when the time is right."

It was his turn to hesitate. "I'll hold you to that."

And he would, but for now Toni knew her friend, and the town's best policeman, would do what she asked.

On to her own research. Where to start? The courthouse? The older citizens in town? Her childhood pediatrician? Maybe the local newspapers would hold what she needed. Or not.

She wouldn't be able to run down to the courthouse today, but she could squeeze in time to make a couple of calls. She ran her finger over the listings in the phone book and punched in the number.

Toni listened to the ring on the other end. At last, just when she expected an answering machine to kick on, someone picked up.

"Merri Ann? This is Toni DeLuca."

"Toni? Danny's girl? How are you, child?"

Child. West Virginia country doctors never allowed their baby patients to grow up. She supposed the nurses held the same view.

"I'm fine, Miss Merri. How's Dr. Phelps?"

Merri Ann's voice lowered. "He's not been

well this week. Has a late fall cold and bronchitis. I'm afraid it's going to turn into pneumonia if he doesn't take better care of himself. You know how stubborn he can be..."

The old nurse rambled on for another five minutes before asking, "What was it you were wanting, child?"

"I thought maybe I could come by some day this week and pick Dr. Felly's brain."

Merri Ann chuckled, and Toni knew she enjoyed her use of Dr. Phelps' nickname.

"I know he'd love to see you, but he's just not up to it. Why not give me a call in a couple days?"

Toni rang off and heaved a deep sigh. If the old dear hadn't been so sick she would have begged for permission to search his files. As much as she wanted to, she couldn't bother them with it right now. And asking Merri Ann questions about her birth would be the same as broadcasting the news to the entire town. No. She'd wait until she could talk with Dr. Felly personally.

Forty minutes later, after doing a quick search on the internet for the DeLuca's and coming up with nothing she didn't already know, she gave up on finding anything about her family. For the time being.

She sat staring at the screen, curiosity playing havoc in her mind. Typing in Perrin's name brought up a list of Douglas far greater than she had time to look into. With narrowing the search she was down to fourteen different Perrin Douglases. Another quick command and she eyed the information across her screen.

Information she already knew or suspected,

lit up the screen, true, but verification for her own nosy self, definitely: University Professor Perrin Douglas. At Ohio State University. A PhD in History with a BA in Ancestry. A long list of papers he wrote as an authority in his subjects. Awards and honorable distinctions he'd received, along with a couple nonfiction books he authored.

Impressive.

She clicked on another link which brought up a picture of his wife and one of their wedding day. A short announcement about the birth of his son.

Nothing to suggest criminal activity. Unless...

She sent the cursor two pages up and reread the article. Could the political rally from his college days count? Perhaps the protest he encouraged a group of students to engineer would label him as a troublemaker.

Or not. Rather lame for a true trouble maker at heart. She sighed. Too bad. She was hoping to find something—anything—that would justify her saying the words, "I thought so."

Roxie called her name and the sharpness in her voice had the alarm bells in her head clanging like a fire station alert.

Toni stuck her head through the doorway and eyed the mother figure, friend and her secretary wrapped in one lavish body.

Roxie covered the phone and motioned frantically at her. "It's Rod. He's calling from the Crawford's. Something's happened. He's put me on hold."

Toni reached across Roxie's desk and hit the speaker button. "Is he okay? The workers?"

Roxie replaced the receiver, her knuckles white and tight. "I don't know."

Seconds passed.

Toni glanced at the wall clock. She had twenty minutes before Perrin Douglas was due here. There was time for her to make a run to the job site and see firsthand what was going on. If she hurried. She stood.

"Roxie, I'm heading out there. Mr. Douglas is due at ten. If I'm not back, tell him I'll call this afternoon and reschedule."

She grabbed her satchel and headed for the door.

"Toni, wait. I think—"

"Better yet, Roxie, use your cell and try to call Mr. Douglas before he gets here so he won't have to make the trip." She held the door open. "If Rod calls, make sure you call me on my cell."

The door slammed behind her.

~*~

The doubts were back in full force—in spite of last evening.

Perrin had to admit it had been pleasant. Last night she'd convinced him—without even knowing it—he'd made the right decision, so he'd allowed himself to forget about his doubts. But the glow radiating from Toni DeLuca and her convincing act had dimmed again in the light of day. Hadn't his experience with Marge taught him anything? He was like a moth that couldn't stay away from the bright zapper light.

Blake had risen earlier than usual. Perrin, in his study, heard his son call out something about a report. Busy trying to get his thirty-second chapter finished, and feeling the pressure of a deadline, Perrin mumbled an answer and forgot about everything but the world he created in his mind, with his fingertips, and on his computer.

The phone rang just as the conflict his protagonist faced increased to a feverish pitch. Perrin ignored it and concentrated on getting the next thought typed. Two minutes later, the ringing started again, and he snatched it up.

"What?" He snapped and gritted his teeth. "I'm busy."

"Mr. Douglas? Is this Perrin Douglas?" The voice had a pronounced country accent.

"Who else would it be at this time of the day? How am I supposed to work with everyone in this town calling me?"

The person on the other end seemed to pay no attention to his growl. "This is Roxie Polinsky from DeLuca's Construction."

"What do you want? I'm not supposed to be there till ten."

"There's been an emergency, and Toni's been called out to the site. She'll ring you this afternoon to reschedule."

"Does she think I'm at her disposal? Is this a delay that will cost me money?" The words slipped out before he could stop himself from attacking this unseen person.

He heard a gasp. Felt the pause. He could almost see her taking a breath, readying herself for the battle—er—reply.

"Mr. Douglas. You're not the only person with valuable time. DeLuca Construction's one of the most respectable businesses in Appleton and has a fine reputation. Everyone loves Toni. I expect you'll find that out after you've been here for awhile." The country twang had disappeared the longer she reprimanded him.

Shame at his rudeness tugged at him. Regardless of having his work disturbed, he didn't have to take it out on her. He did have a tendency to expect time to move around him, and to be fair, he hadn't even spoken to Miss DeLuca about Rita Mae's comments. She should have a chance to defend herself.

If DeLuca's proved to be trustworthy and not the subject of malicious gossip—giving him an excuse to back out of the contract—they might put his project on a back burner till doom's day if they got busy with other work. He couldn't risk it. Diplomacy was called for.

He cleared his throat and crossed mental fingers. "Perhaps I spoke too hastily. I'm sure Miss DeLuca has a good reason to postpone our meeting. I meant no disrespect to either the business or her."

Another pause. He could sense her thoughts and almost see her sniffing out the sound of his apology for sincerity. Had he been too formal? More than likely, given his lack of social abilities.

"Very well. I'll tell Toni you'll expect her call."

Perrin let out his breath and grimaced. He forced himself not to slam the phone down. With a watchdog like that, Toni DeLuca needed no other guard.

He glanced at his computer screen. Where was he?

His last thought gone, mind whirling from a hundred different things, he focused on the last line he'd typed.

Huge brown eyes with golden flecks in them, eyes that danced with life, teased him.

Perrin frowned and pressed his finger on the backspace key. Where had that come from? Why was he describing Toni DeLuca in his manuscript?

He wished it was as easy to erase the thought of her from his mind as easily as he erased words from the screen.

Chapter Six

Toni pushed the speed limit as she swerved through the traffic.

God, let Rod and the guys be okay.

Nervous tension teased at her stomach when she finally caught sight of the Crawford property. She pulled straight up to the job and jumped out, giving the door a shove behind herself. She saw Rod bent over something.

Rod turned his head, straightened, and called out, "Toni."

"What is it? Is everyone okay?"

"Afraid not. Shawn climbed up onto the scaffolding, and it collapsed." Rod spoke in an undertone. "He's hurt pretty badly, I think."

Toni moved to the young man and took his hand. "You in pain?"

"Not too bad, Miss Toni."

The grimace said otherwise.

Rod straightened. "Here's the EMS now."

Boss and Supervisor watched as the experienced team prepared, loaded, and pulled away, sirens blaring.

Rod picked up a bar, pointed at the damaged sections. "Look."

Toni touched it, felt the jagged edges. Had one of these pieces been used as her attacker's weapon the other night? "It's been sawed."

"Not only that one, but several others have had a saw taken to them. Just enough that they gave under pressure." He scratched his head, his angry voice brisk, and his lips thin with tension.

Toni looked around. Had kids done this? She'd never had trouble with competitors but...? Many of the neighboring towns had had more than their share of pranks that caused quite a bit of damage. So far Appleton had been fortunate to escape.

Her other three workers stood milling around, their gazes on her, their faces sober and watchful. All except Kevin. Toni eyed her newest employee, Kevin. He seemed unusually restless. Or was it nervousness?

"Anyone know anything?" Toni met their gaze with a sober expression. "Seen anything?"

Heads shook.

Toni turned to Rod. "You call the cops?"

"Not yet."

"Please do it, Rod. We need to get to the bottom of this as quickly as we can." Toni shivered at the thought of what could have happened. She stared at the tall end-piece sections still standing.

"One other thing, Toni."

She swung around, the pounding in her chest just a bit heavier.

"This was tied onto a stretch of the scaffolding."

Her gaze dipped from his face to his hands, and she flinched. He held out a small pink card, and she took it.

No words. Just a round, hand-drawn picture of a smiling face.

Did she have the strength to bend over and pick her heart up? She had to. Her men were staring at her. Probably wondering...She had to pull herself together.

She plastered a smile onto her lips. "The police will be here soon. Be as cooperative as you can."

An hour and half later, Deputy Eddy Snider confirmed what Toni had seen. The scaffolding had been sawn.

Eddy shook his head, his droopy eyes on the construction site. "We're not going to get much here." He gave Toni an apologetic look. "You know we're not equipped for in-depth forensics, unless you want us to call in the state lab. But you know I'll do what I can."

Toni tilted her head back and squeezed her eyes shut. That would mean more money spent cause their town sure didn't have that kind of cash.

The sun warmed her face, but her heart ached with coldness. Why was this happening? Those hateful cards were distressing enough, but someone tampering with her equipment? Hurting her employees?

A hand touched her shoulder, and she opened her eyes to see Rod squinting at her in the bright sunlight.

"Hey, it's okay, kiddo. We'll get through this."

"I know." Her voice croaked. She cleared her throat and gave him a lopsided grin. "Just some extra things going on right now."

Rod studied her face for a moment. "Anything you need to talk over with Uncle Rod?"

"Go on with you. I'm okay." Did her laugh sound as fake to him as it did to her? "Will you give the hospital a quick call after while to check on Shawn? I'll drop by this evening and take him some flowers."

She opened her truck door then turned back to her supervisor. "What kind of recommendation did Kevin have when we hired him?"

Rod's brows drew together. "Pretty good. Is there something I should know about?"

"Not sure yet, but I'll let you know if something develops. Thanks, Rod."

As Toni drove herself back to the office, questions pounded in her mind. What was it about? Someone after something? Vengeance for a wrong?

Toni blinked. As far as she knew, she'd not harmed anyone. She loved—or at least tolerated—everyone in her beloved Appleton.

There was no way it was kids. Not with that laughing face on the note. Aimed at her, and taunting.

Although Rod was the one who worked with her employees and dealt with them on a daily basis, she was the boss, passed out the paychecks every week, inquired about their families, and sent presents to their kids. She loved their loyalty to her and DeLuca Construction, even during the thin times. Loved how they respected her and worked hard.

But she was responsible for their having work. For their pay. For their protection.

A wave of depression pressed in on her, threatening to draw her into its pool.

As she entered the office, she asked, "You talk with Rod?"

Her secretary nodded.

"Then get me Perrin Douglas's number, will you? I need to reschedule."

"Why not do it this evening? Meet him at Apple Blossoms?"

"*As a date?*" Roxie was a real schemer when it came to Toni's love life. She couldn't count all the times the woman had tried to hook her up with this man or that one. "I don't think so."

"Ah, Toni, come on. You need to relax a bit. Besides, I'm thinking about *him*. I'm sure it will ease the tension in him."

Did Roxie know something she didn't? Probably.

"I'm sure you are." She eyed her friend. What she said made sense, and, well, why not? She could use the relaxation. It would give her a chance to see Starli and maybe improve Douglas's mood. Hmmm.

"Okay. You win." She laughed as Roxie visibly gloated. "I'll stop on the way to the restaurant to see how Shawn's doing, then deal with our newest client. I just hope he doesn't steal my appetite with his complaints."

"Don't let *him* get to you." The emphasis on the word him gave Toni pause.

"I won't. I plan to call him as soon as you quit talking, get me his number, and I can get to my desk phone."

Roxie's slack-jawed expression forced Toni to question her. "Okay, what did you do?"

Her secretary looked down, her cheeks as rosy as the Red Delicious apple Toni had brought to work that morning.

"I didn't do anything but what you asked me

to."

Toni crossed her arms and tapped a foot. "Yeah, right. 'Fess up."

"I gave him some very much needed motherly advice."

Toni eyed her, suspicion edging her thoughts.

Roxie hastened to assure her. "Of course, I let him know you'd be calling this afternoon to reschedule. I'm sure he'll be quite cooperative."

"Why do I feel like I'm getting the truth, but not the whole truth?" Toni lifted her hands in surrender, and marched into her office. She heard Roxie's raucous laughter as she slammed her door.

Toni shuffled papers until Roxie finally had the number. Perrin picked up the phone after the second ring.

"Hi, it's Toni DeLuca, calling to reschedule."

"Your...secretary said something about an emergency. Is everything all right?"

Had he hesitated after that "your"? Toni sighed. Roxie. She obviously had said something very pointed to the man.

"A few problems here and there."

"You need to postpone another day?"

Toni held the phone receiver away from her ear. Had she heard him right? He was being very nice. "No. No, of course not. I'm calling to see if you'd like to meet this evening? I'm sorry about this morning and would like to make it up to you. You know how things go."

She was rambling. She held out a hand. Nope. No shakes. Then why did her stomach feel like a bowl full of quivering gelatin?

She'd try again. "I'm inviting you to dinner.

A business dinner, of course. Apple Blossoms is a semiformal restaurant at the edge of our downtown. Live music, super food. We can discuss your project then if you wish."

"Dinner, huh? Tomorrow won't work for me, so I guess tonight is it. All right. I accept. I do want to go over a couple things with you."

After agreeing to meet him at the restaurant at 7:30, Toni hung up and gathered her things. She peered at Roxie as she headed out, and couldn't stop the grin. "I'm out to check that concrete the guys did Monday. Do me a favor, will you? Call for reservations at Blossoms. And make it for two."

What better way to investigate a suspect than to socialize?

~*~

Today had been a disaster. If he had very many more days filled with interruptions, he'd never meet his deadline. Yet he couldn't blame it all on the secretary. His own mind had been on the curly-headed owner of DeLuca Construction. Had someone really thrown that rock at her house, or was it a play for some agenda of hers?

That trembling lip last night troubled him more than he wanted to admit. He wished he knew whether she was a superb actress or a scared woman.

Perrin sat back, set the cup of lukewarm coffee on his desk and grimaced. He'd have to make a fresh pot soon. His gaze took in his computer screen, the research papers tacked to a large bulletin board, and finally settled on the view outside his window.

Appleton had seemed an ideal choice for his

writing. Quiet, good schools, and people who minded their own business and let him get on with his.

All he'd wanted was to have his addition built and be left alone so he could finish his book. No women to intrude into his life. Only his work. And Blake, of course.

But enter Toni DeLuca, with her bubbling personality and business sense. And now, by the sound of it, problems before they'd even begun the job.

He frowned. To be fair, it wasn't her fault he had a problem with trusting women in general. He blamed Marge—and himself—for his distrust. But on top of that, had been the phone call from the brass secretary, informing him of the first postponement. And who could tell how many more there might be? What could go wrong? Delayed deliveries of material? Accidents? Disagreements and refusals to take his suggestions?

Now the owner calling him for a dinner date. Rather, a business date, and he did need to question her, but still, just like a woman. Exactly how Marge acted when she'd wanted something. He shouldn't have accepted, should have insisted on meeting at her office, but since he'd already snapped up her invitation like a lovesick puppy and had time to reflect on it, he'd remain cool and detached.

Toni DeLuca, with those lips made for kissing. Perrin felt his stomach quiver and frowned. He had to admit, no longer than he'd known her, she was a multi-talented woman, a person with diverse tastes and interests. A person deserving of admiration. If it'd been just her looks—he could fight that. But he had no idea how to win against such confidence from a woman both smart and gentle.

He groaned. A whole evening with her, trying to stay aloof. An evening listening to her chatter about her business. Or what she thought ought to be done with his addition. Or how his ideas could be changed...and on and on and on.

Perrin shoved his glasses onto his nose. No, he wasn't looking forward to tonight.

Chapter Seven

Toni whirled in front of her mirror and admired the coral and cream flowered skirt of her dress as it ballooned out from her legs. She grinned at her mirror image and made a gamin face.

Whoop-dee-doo. She was as excited as if this was her first date. Only it wasn't. It wasn't even a date, per se. It was a business dinner with a person she suspected wanted to destroy her business. A person she hardly knew, let alone trusted. Period.

It had been awhile since she'd been out with a man. What with her father dying and her taking over the reins of the business, she'd been far too busy to pay serious attention to any men who were in the vicinity. Two years had passed in a blur of work.

Not that there'd been anyone who'd caught her fancy the last few years. Toby Gibson, years ago, had indicated interest, but he was like a brother.

And there was Arnie who was a nice enough guy, and who was constantly after her to go here or there. Rather, Sylvia, his mother, continually shoved her son at her.

Appleton, for all its country charm, ran short on available men.

When her spirits had dipped this morning,

she'd grabbed—at Roxie's insistence—her courage and proposed dinner with the first man she'd found interesting in a long time. Blame it on business or her suspicions all she wanted. She knew the truth. She only wished her suspicions ruled her, instead of interests. How weak could a girl be?

She touched her hair. Of course, she wasn't considering anyone in a romantic way. Especially a long-term relationship. Not even a short-term one. She liked her life just the way it was, thank you, very much. No way did she want it interrupted by a man, especially a good-looking one, who had emotional problems way too big for her to handle. Besides, she had enough to do handling her own problems.

Toni picked up her lace shawl, gave the calico a few strokes, then left in her Mustang.

~*~

Shawn didn't look so hot as Toni tiptoed to his bedside. Several different tubes and a beeping monitor sent her heart to her throat. If looks were anything to go by, he'd not be here on this earth long. Tears pricked her lids.

"T-o-n-i."

The breathless whisper had her shaking her head to throw off the tears blinding her sight.

"Shawn. How are you?"

"Pretty...good, I think. Better than...morning."

She wanted to agree he looked better, but it wasn't true.

"I brought you some flowers."

"N-i-c-e. Thanks."

"You're not to worry about anything. Roxie double checked, and you're covered under our insurance."

He moved his head.

"Is there anything I can do?"

The young man frowned. He was covered in bandages, but she could tell by the way his lips thinned that something bothered him.

"What's wrong?"

"No-thing...me. Need...check out...Kevin. And Sssowww...Heard..."

Kevin? So someone else had questions about him. Rod reported he kept to himself, mostly, but was an excellent worker, never slacking. He wasn't exactly what anyone called friendly, a bit on the morose side, truth be told. As Rod insisted though, they could live with that, given his work habit.

So why did Shawn want him checked out? Had he seen something?

And who or what was 'Ssss'?

Toni focused on her bed-ridden employee again, but he'd drifted off to sleep. Patting his hand, she whispered a quick prayer and exited the room.

Time to pull Rod into the loop.

~*~

Apple Blossoms was as elegant as ever, the Christmas décor as classical as the restaurant owner.

After parking, she walked inside and spotted Perrin immediately. His tailored tan corduroy jacket and dark brown pants a perfect fit. His light blue shirt and diamond patterned tie brought out the beautiful blue-green of his eyes behind his glasses. The most gorgeous eyes she'd ever seen.

Unfortunately, the two women, standing

next to him and chatting as if they'd always known him, dampened her excitement. When had Perrin met Sylvia and her disagreeable friend, Rita Mae?

Toni slowed her progress across the floor, tempted to bolt from the restaurant. Fortunately, her natural tenacity at facing difficulty kicked in. So what if her business client talked with people she wasn't super fond of? Who knew when and why Perrin had met them?

And really, who cared? She definitely shouldn't.

Her inward wince gave her away, at least to herself.

"Hi. You look great." Yikes. What kind of comment was that, especially in front of Rita Mae and Sylvia? So much for remaining neutral. The snickers from the other two didn't help any.

Perrin smiled, one side of his mouth quirking up, a devastatingly cute dimple in his left cheek. His gaze traveled over her outfit, then rose to meet her eyes again. "I think that's supposed to be my line. You look pretty glamorous yourself."

All her thoughts froze as she stood mesmerized by his eyes. Yet, was there something behind his eyes, lurking, waiting on her reaction? To what? She shook off her mental paralysis.

He looked down, then raised the flowers he held. "These are for you."

Flowers? Why would he buy her flowers? She hesitated, thrilled at his gentlemanly act, stunned at his thoughtfulness, suspicious of his motive.

A hand stretched out to—what? Pluck one from the bunch? But she reached for them before Sylvia's hand could succeed. Electricity zipped through her fingers as they touched his. She could hear the stiffness in her voice as she spoke. "Thanks. You didn't have to do this."

"Of course, he didn't, Silly." Sylvia flouted. "When will you learn some social manners? If only you'd listen, you'd learn a lot from Arnie."

It gave her no satisfaction to hold back the retort Toni wanted to slap at the blond rebuking her. Instead she layered her remark with a bit of honey, hoping to defuse Sylvia's usual complaints. "Arnie does have superb manners."

Sylvia simpered at her, but cast a glance at Perrin. "Thanks to his mama."

~*~

Perrin's heart skipped a beat when the doorman swung open the heavy wooden door, and Toni walked in looking like an exotic flower in a coral-colored dress. She was beautiful, and he was suddenly glad he'd followed through on his instinct to stop for the flowers at a stand.

So much for cool and detached. He knew he was staring, but he couldn't take his eyes off her. The two women in front of him were chatting, each vying for his attention. He half-listened, giving the proper responses, but his whole focus was on the woman moving toward him.

She'd done something to her hair. Down, luxuriously full, and pulled back on one side, her almost black curls were fastened with some kind of glittery comb. Her skin glowed with the slight tan of her Italian heritage. And with that name he knew it had to be Italian.

He shifted, feeling suddenly awkward. In almost a panic, he bid Rita Mae and her friend a good evening and ignored their light protests as they moved away.

Toni handed over and requested a vase for the flowers from a passing waiter. But was that a veil shielding her eyes from their true emotion? Maybe he shouldn't have bought them. It was too much. Another gaffe, and laughable. When was the last time he'd bought flowers for a woman? Four years? Three, for sure. It'd been for Marge, before she'd...

Toni wasn't laughing. Her face, relaxed and serene, was tinted pink to match her dress. That inferiority complex Marge had left him with, was playing another mean trick.

He spoke in a low voice as they walked toward the dining room. "I assume you made reservations."

"Of course." Toni turned as an outlandishly tall, thin man with styled, gray hair approached. "Manny."

"Miss Toni, how are you? It's been a while since you've been here." His affectionate chiding tone didn't quite match the sharp glance he gave her. "Are you all right? You look..."

"I'm fine, Manny. Stop your fussing." She craned her neck to see around his frame. "Did you save my favorite table? Is Starli here tonight?"

Manny's white teeth flashed in a broad smile. "Do you think Miss Starli would allow me to live if I did not make sure everything was perfect for her dearest friend?"

Toni clasped the waiter's arm. "She adores you, and you know it. She'd never fire you."

Perrin watched the interaction between the two and listened as they chatted like friends. When Manny led them to a secluded table by a large floor-to-ceiling window, Toni still clutching the waiter's arm, he followed. Once seated, Manny took their drink orders and disappeared.

"I assume Starli is the owner?"

"She is. It's a beautiful place, isn't it?"

"Yes. Did you drive your purple truck?"

Her lips widened in a friendly smile. "I drove my Mustang."

"A Mustang?"

She nodded, and silken curls bounced against her cheek. "I have a classic."

"Besides your purple truck? What kind?"

"It's a '69, slant-back, cherry red Mustang with a black vinyl top, scoop, and a 428 super cobra, police interceptor engine. Gorgeous and powerful." She cocked her head. "And my truck isn't purple. It's violet."

Perrin looked at this girl and wondered who she was.

Classy woman, smart business owner, casual construction worker, simple homemaker, or Italian princess? "You rolled that description off your tongue like you've done it before. Don't tell me you race cars, too."

Her laughter was musical and full-hearted. "Well...I drag-raced a few times before I took over my daddy's business, but I'm too busy now."

Perrin sat back and crossed his legs, his interest building. "Who are you?"

Her eyes glittered at him, her lips widened in a mischievous grin.

"But a woman drag racing? The men here accept that?"

"Why not?" She snickered at his skeptical look. "The truth is, the local drag racers accepted me only because they knew and respected dad. Hassling Danny DeLuca's daughter might have made for a higher bid the next time one of the guys needed work done to his spiffy house."

"Bribery and all that."

"Actually, Daddy knew after a taste of the excitement, I'd be ready to return to my more feminine side. I like beautiful things and..." she cast him a quick glance "...love to dress up."

"Total opposites."

"What? Construction and drag racing and frilly, feminine clothes?"

The teasing note in her voice rang strong. She was in high spirits tonight.

"There's nothing better to pick up my spirits than a night on the town. Oh, good. Reverend Burke and his group are playing."

Startled at her quick change of subject, Perrin cast a glance at the stage. He'd heard the vibrant music when they'd entered but paid no attention. Now he saw a band of six men and one woman on a small-sized stage.

"What are they playing?"

"It's an old, old spiritual. 'Swing Low, Sweet Chariot.' They specialize in them, a little jazz, and a few of the softer, easy listening love songs." Toni swayed to the music. "They're chanting now."

"Chanting?"

"Call and response."

When he sent her a confused look, Toni went on, "Reverend Burke's calling, the others are responding. Listen."

Reverend Burke sang, "Swing low, sweet chariot..."

His backup crooned, "Coming for to carry me home."

"I thought West Virginians only listened to hillbilly music." He nodded toward the musicians.

"It's called Appalachian, and they do. It's quite entertaining and has a lot of lyrical meaning. Listen to it when you get the chance, and it might actually change your tune."

Perrin didn't give her a direct answer. "Why is this place so classy then if most of the residents like country?"

"Country music doesn't mean we're hicks. Some of us even made it through high school."

Great. His snobbishness was showing. Again. "Sorry, I really didn't mean to be offensive. I guess if I'm going to live here, I'd better learn to be a little more tolerant."

"I guess you'd better."

That was direct enough. He cleared his throat. "Do they play every night of the week?"

"No." Toni shook her head.

Perrin found his gaze fixated on her curls.

"Tuesdays and Thursdays, she has another small band. A husband and wife couple play the sax and guitar sometimes, and Starli plays the piano on days whenever one of the groups need a break."

Perrin nodded. "The place is certainly attractive enough. Now if the food lives up to it."

"Oh, it will." Confidence registered in her voice.

A hand touched his shoulder. Patted. A voice crooned in his ear. A strong feminine perfume smell assaulted his nose. "Perrin. I forgot to remind you. You haven't stopped in at The Specialty House. Bad boy."

Bad boy?

Toni was biting her lips. Was she upset?

Perrin pulled away slowly and turned.

Rita Mae Simpson leaned in closer.

"I've been a little busy—"

"Too busy for some of my famous Mocha coffee?" Another pat. She slid a side-ways glance at Toni and smirked. "I've been a little— uh, preoccupied myself. But I'm never too busy for handsome men. Come by in the morning and your coffee's on me."

"Sounds good. I'll see what I can do."

She winked and cast a wide-eyed stare at him. "Come over. I want you to meet someone."

Perrin cast a quick glance at Toni. Her eyes betrayed her feelings of amused contempt. A narrow shoulder lifted.

He wished she'd not been so nonchalant with her agreement. He'd make this quick. "You sure? I won't be a minute."

"Go. I'll sit and enjoy the music. Starli will be out soon to greet her guests."

He nodded. "The owner."

"And one of my best friends."

"I won't be long." Perrin allowed Rita Mae to

clasp his arm and steer them through a maze of white cloth-covered tables.

Still ten feet from her friends, Rita Mae called out. "Look who I stole from—"

Perrin turned toward her, and she stopped.

"—for a few minutes, and he's a writer. Let him see my new brochures, Kevin.

Perrin unfolded it. Attractive. Whoever worked on it had done a good job. "I like it. Concise, but enough info to attract attention."

Ecstatic, Rita crowed to her companions. "What did I tell you? He knows his stuff."

One pair of male eyes narrowed.

Someone else didn't trust him.

~*~

Toni watched the two walk away and approach Rita Mae's companions on the opposite side of the restaurant.

Sylvia, sitting at the table, eyed them as they approached and didn't look one bit pleased. At Perrin? Or, with the way Rita Mae clutched the man's arm as if she owned him?

One of the men scribbled on a piece of paper and hastily stuffed it inside his jacket when someone beside him spoke. She couldn't see that second man, only his suited arm and the very edge of his head.

She didn't know the first man, but he was good looking in a distinguished way. When he glanced up at the two approaching the table, Toni caught a glimpse of his eyes before Perrin and Rita Mae blocked her view. They were the eyes of a man who'd seen too much.

What was he doing with Rita Mae and Sylvia?

Chapter Eight

"Is she for real? Or is all that an act?"

Toni sighed. "That's our Rita Mae. Never fails to try her charms on every new man in town."

Conflicting opinions. Rita Mae's and Toni's. Rita Mae warning him of Toni's business problems and Toni, silent, but just as capably indicating her dislike of Rita Mae. Which one had the correct viewpoint? Or were they both, as women, equally wrong?

"I wanted to speak with you about a couple of things."

Toni's gaze moved from his face to behind him, and hers lit up.

He turned and caught a glimpse of a tall, white-blond woman gliding toward them. Manny, following the young woman, carried a tray high in the air with one hand, deftly avoiding any possible collisions.

Toni rose as the woman called out in a soft voice. They embraced and exchanged several comments before Toni made the introductions and added, "He's just moved to Appleton with his son, Blake."

Starli tilted her head at Perrin and motioned for Manny to serve their drinks. "Please. Let's sit." She studied Perrin for a moment with beautiful green eyes.

Too green to suit him. Reminded him of...emeralds. The stone Marge had loved.

"What do you do, Mr. Douglas?"

"I'm a college professor. Taught for fifteen years at Ohio State."

"And now?"

Perrin hesitated. Her cool tone suggested she didn't like him, but he had no clue why she would feel that way. As far as he knew he'd never met the ice maiden before. Must be the night to meet people who mistrusted him.

"I've taken a hiatus for five years to finish some projects I've planned to do."

"And your wife? What does she do?" Two pairs of eyes stared at him. Demanded an answer.

An electric surge of anger ran from his stomach to his brain, blinding him of any reasonable reply, scorching him from any decent emotional response. Perrin returned her stare, biting back the one word he wanted to spit out.

Dead.

Starli opened her mouth, and Perrin assumed she was ready with another impossible question, but at that moment Manny slipped up beside Toni and handed her a folded paper.

Reprieved. The intense attention veered away from him, and it was just as well. He had no desire to be rude, but neither was he about to spill the details of his life to these two women.

Perrin took a sip of his sparkling cider and then another. He'd better watch it. His head had been in a cloud from the moment Toni

DeLuca had walked through the restaurant door. He'd almost forgotten the real intent of this dinner meeting. The questions he needed to ask. The reassurance he wanted that his decision to hire DeLuca Construction had been the right one.

Toni took the paper and glanced up at the headwaiter, her brow raised. "For me?"

The tall man leaned down to murmur in her ear, but the words carried, and Perrin had no trouble hearing. "It was left at one of the tables, addressed to you, and the server gave it to me. I thought perhaps you'd want it."

"You don't know who left it?"

Manny cleared his throat. "No. But I will discover that information."

Toni flashed him a smile and nodded. "Thanks, Manny."

She tossed Starli and him an apologetic look and unfolded the page. Her tan skin went white.

Perrin narrowed his eyes and set his glass down carefully. Something was wrong. He glanced at Starli Cameron, then back to Toni who still hadn't looked up.

"Toni?"

Perrin's gaze whipped back to Toni's friend.

"Are you all right?" Starli leaned forward to touch Toni's hand.

When Toni lifted her gaze, the stricken look on her face sent a wave of déjà-vue over Perrin. How many times had he felt that end-of-the-world feeling?

Starli was on her feet and beside Toni in an instant. Panic bordered her voice. "What is it? Toni, dear. Tell me..."

"I'm okay. I'm okay. Sit down, Starli."

Perrin's gaze circled the room, then stopped at the doorway. A man was just turning away, and if he wasn't mistaken, that was a smile plastered on his narrow face. What had Rita Mae said the man was called? Not Kevin Meyers. Sal something or the other.

The color seeped back into Toni's face and in seconds she was smiling again.

Whatever had been the problem, he'd just better remember that as attractive as Toni was, he had no time—no desire—for a relationship with her. Or anyone.

Never again.

~*~

Manny returned to their table. "Miss Toni. The last party at that table was a group of four. I don't know the names of the two gentlemen, but Rita Mae Simpson reserved the table. Her friend Sylvia Searles was with her."

Starli and she exchanged glances as Manny backed away. Her gaze flicked to Perrin. His blue green eyes darkened. Was he wondering about her thoughts and hoping she didn't foster anything suspicious about him?

She'd seen Rita Mae's table and her companions. Well, all of them but the one shielded by that large fern. So who had that been? And which one of them had blatantly left such a message?

Toni chatted with her friend for ten minutes, wanting to assure her that she was fine. She knew they'd have to talk soon, but not tonight. Not with Perrin here.

In spite of her assurances to her best friend and to Perrin Douglas, her heart felt as if it'd been ripped in two pieces.

The first shock had passed, true. If what the paper said was true, someone had proof. Proof about her dad. Proof that she was...

Was that someone Rita Mae? Had she left the message?

And the forever, ongoing question: was all this connected—the threatening notes, the damages at the construction sites, and Shawn's injury?

Twisted in between all the strands of worry, were her thoughts about the man sitting across from her. What had he thought? He'd not said a word and asked no questions.

He'd been friendly from the minute she'd walked in to meet him. But she'd sensed the moment he'd withdrawn—when Starli had questioned him. As if he didn't want to talk about his past life. As if he had something to hide.

For the first time she could ever remember, Toni wished Starli would excuse herself. She shifted in her seat. She sure didn't need any more minutes alone with this fascinating man.

But needing and wanting were two different things.

~*~

She was almost home when the lights from the vehicle behind her caught her attention in the rearview mirror. Were they the same lights that had been behind her all the way? Had Perrin followed her to make sure she was all right?

But why would he do that? She hadn't indicated she needed protection, had she? Of course not. What was there to be afraid of in

Appleton, West Virginia? The small town where nothing of real importance happened. Ever. Except, of course, the threats she'd received. And Shawn's accident. And...

There was no way to tell who it was, but they were following way too close. Way too...

The bump was light and quick, and then the vehicle backed off. Had to be a car. A big car but smaller than a truck. A truck would have towered over her Mustang.

Still, she winced as she imagined the damage. She was almost home. Another block...

Her gaze was riveted on the mirror as the car raced up behind her, and this time it wasn't a light tap. Her body slammed forward, then back, but the seat belt kept her from ramming into the steering wheel or worse. Pressing her foot on the gas, her Mustang sprang forward and outdistanced the car for half a block. Then as she was within feet of her own drive, it came tearing up behind her, and Toni tensed.

With a force she hadn't experienced, it rammed into her car, and sent it headlong into the wooden fence surrounding her property. She didn't stop until her bumper smashed into the front porch sending one pillar backward into the wall, rolling down until it crashed onto the porch floor.

Toni sat dazed, and then as porch lights flipped on from nearby neighbors, she thrust open her door and fell out grabbing hold of the car roof to gaze at the idling car still in the street.

She didn't recognize it, but it looked

ominous—big and black and scary, not knowing who sat behind the tinted windows, who'd tried to harm her. Or was it more accurate to say, kill her?

Squinting, she realized it was an older car, a Buick, maybe, or a Caddy, and definitely a four door. There was no way to see the license plate, but that white stripe that ran from the front fender to the back stood out like a canary pretending to be an eagle.

He must have spotted her because with a roar, the car tore down the road and disappeared around a corner, its tires screeching a little bit, the body rocking as if the suspension was bad.

Toni sank to the tilting edge of her porch and drew in deep breaths of air. Her palm pressed against an aching cheek.

What on earth was going on?

~*~

Perrin woke early. Out of sorts, he plodded to the kitchen and started to prepare his morning coffee and stopped. Rita Mae had practically made him promise last night to stop in at her shop for coffee this morning. And why not? Maybe for a short time, it would take his mind off the increasing attraction he felt for the owner of the company he'd hired days ago.

His desk beckoned as he went to dress, but he ignored it. After last night, he doubted he could concentrate this early anyhow.

Forty minutes later, he shoved open the door of Appleton Specialty Coffees and almost bumped into Toni DeLuca.

~*~

Toni pulled out of her garage Saturday

morning with the signed contract from Perrin Douglas in her briefcase. She scowled as she drove.

Her head ached, her whole body was stiff and sore. Worse, the sky rumbled and brooded, threatening rain.

Why wouldn't she feel like death warmed over? After last night's fiasco, she had a right to feel a little disgruntled.

And just because the man who'd hired her company to build for him had turned emotional meant nothing to her. Hadn't she known from that first day he could be a problem? She'd tried to be friendly and show him she could keep her word. And if he was pouting, well, it wasn't her fault they'd never gotten around to discussing business. The trouble was, her interest in him was developing faster than she could keep up with. It did no good to reason with her heart. It refused to listen.

Toni brushed at the tears that stung her eyes. No wonder Starli had vowed to never marry again. Men. Who could understand them?

Except Daddy, of course. She flinched as doubts intruded. The first she'd ever had.

Did she know the man she'd called Daddy for thirty-two years as much as she'd thought she had? Worse, did these recent doubts have something to do with the damages at DeLuca's construction site jobs? Or the accusing cards? Or the attack last night?

Time to squeeze in a cup of Rita Mae's specialty coffee. As much as she disliked the woman, her coffee was the best in the state.

Toni parked and dashed to the door of the café. She saw no sign of the owner and was grateful for small favors. The place was full. Sylvia Searles and that handsome man she'd been with last night huddled at a table for two and studied some papers scattered around their coffee cups.

Placing her order, she tapped her fingers, hoping to leave before Rita Mae showed up. When the waiter finally handed her the steaming brew, she dashed toward the door...and almost ran down the man entering.

Looking up, she grimaced, then caught herself. Perrin Douglas stared down at her, but nothing in his expression showed anymore delight than she felt.

Coming for an early coffee like herself? Or hoping to talk with the vivacious owner a little more?

She gave him a curt nod and hurried out, splashing a drop or two of the hot liquid on her fingers. It didn't hurt any more than her heart did.

~*~

Thank God she'd had the sense to keep moving at the coffee shop. Granted, she'd probably seemed crazy, rushing past Perrin like she had, but really? Why would he think she'd want to stop and chit chat when he'd been so cold at the end of last night?

But enough thinking about *that man*. She had work to do.

She was headed downtown. If she wanted real proof—wanted to put these crazy accusations to rest, she needed to find out more. To quit dawdling. Temporarily denied speaking with Dr. Felly, she decided to try the courthouse. It might shed some light. She'd drop off the contract, then stop at the vital statistics department.

The figure of a young man caught her eye, his ungainly, loping stride coaxing a grin from Toni. Blake Douglas. The boy's shoulders hunched under the weight of the oversized duffel bag

She pulled alongside him and tapped her horn.

When he looked toward her, recognition registered in his eyes. He lifted a hand and stepped to the truck, dropping the heavy-looking duffel to the ground.

"Hi. How's things?"

"Okay. Did you and my dad have a good time last night?"

That was to the point. "Very."

She wasn't about to tell him how disappointing the last part of the evening had been. Better concentrate on the first half. "Your dad's an interesting man."

"He's okay."

"You think a lot of him, don't you?" Toni teased.

The skin around his eyes crinkled as he laughed.

"We'll be starting your dad's job next week."

"I told him you were the best." Blake's voice trailed off as his gaze focused on something besides her. One hand ran through his hair, rumpling it. "Who is that?"

"Who is who?" Toni turned to look in the direction he stared, but saw no one.

He shook his head. "Never mind. They're

gone. I've seen that person a couple different times." He shrugged.

Toni studied his face and wondered what had happened to the boy's mother.

"You didn't say where you were going."

Another elaborate shrug. His gaze flew back to her face. "Out to the lake, I guess. Sid's gone with his parents for the weekend. Thought I might feed the ducks for awhile."

He gave his duffel a gentle kick. "Bread for them. Lunch for me."

"Looks awfully heavy."

"Well, I've got a camera, my digging tools, a couple of books, and a few other things."

"Digging tools?"

"Yeah, you know that spot where everyone's always hunting for Indian artifacts and arrowheads?"

"Of course, the Shawnee Mounds."

"I'm sorta interested in archeology."

"Looks like rain."

He cast an accusing glare at the low-hanging black clouds then turned his gaze on her. "You wouldn't want to eat at Rosita's, would you?"

"I thought you packed lunch?"

Another shrug. "The ducks can eat it. I'd rather eat with you."

"I've got work to do first."

"Where you going?"

"To the courthouse to look up some records."

"Sounds boring." He yawned.

"Gotta be done." She cocked her head at him. "I guess I could if you're sure your dad won't mind."

"He won't."

~*~

Perrin jumped up for the fifth time that morning and poured himself another cup of coffee. Then holding it, he paced through the house. His free hand ran through his hair.

The tsunami of feelings surging in his body threatened to overwhelm him. Why had he treated Toni so rudely last night as if she was at fault for his own shortcomings? He definitely had no right to forget, and no right to enjoy the evening as he had. He shouldn't be feeling an attraction to a beautiful woman who didn't know whom she was with. The best thing he could do was stay away from Toni DeLuca.

Perrin stopped his pacing, sloshing a little of the coffee onto his oak floor.

Where was Blake? He thought he could remember him yelling something about going somewhere, but he'd been in the middle of a scene and had scarcely paid any attention.

Blake would have his cell phone. He could call him. Go out for a sub at lunch.

Maybe he could forget for just a little while.

Chapter Nine

Toni shut the last unwieldy book and stacked it with the others the clerk had provided for her. Nothing. Why was there no trace of her birth record? Though the worker had assured her there were no more record books, Toni had eyed the woman and wondered. Her answer had seemed too hurried, her voice too breathless.

Still, Toni suspected, her own feelings played a major role in how she was viewing everything and everyone. She'd have to lighten up with the suspicious nature.

Or not.

She glanced at the big black wall clock. It was five minutes before noon. The pizza place they'd decided on was a ten-minute walk.

She left her truck and headed that way, glad to see the clouds scattering and a cautious sun peeking from behind the few lingering ones.

Blake stood inside, focused on one of the arcade games. She watched him as he played, then heard a cell phone ring.

With a last jam of the sticks, Blake rummaged in the duffel at his feet and pulled it out, sliding a finger across the front, all in one move. "Hey, Dad. What's goin' on?"

Toni walked a few steps away, giving him some privacy in case he wanted it. She caught his glance toward her.

"I'm at Rosita's. I told you this morning I was gonna go to the lake."

Another pause.

"Yeah, I did."

He turned his back to her, the cell pressed against his ear.

"Nope. I mean, No, I'm not by myself."

The boy frowned. "I'm not a baby, Dad. And I did tell you. I've got a friend here with me."

The boy sat up, and his face lit. "Sure. You're not writing this afternoon? Cool. We'll wait. Hey, Dad, hurry, will you?"

He gave a final whoop before tossing his cell back into the duffel.

"Dad's on his way. He should be here in fifteen minutes."

Waves of anticipation rippled through Toni's body. "Did your dad know I was here?"

His smile reached from ear to ear. Mischief lingered in his eyes. "Nope. We'll surprise him." He dropped in a coin for another game.

A surprise for Perrin Douglas. Huh. She had a suspicion that after last night, he wouldn't consider it a good surprise.

~*~

Perrin started to reach for his car keys then looked down at his jeans and grimaced.

At his closet he caught sight of the clear plastic storage box holding the folded clothes he hadn't touched for three and a half years. He stared at them. Why had he kept them?

They'd been some of Marge's favorites, items she picked out for him. Unwanted clothes too flashy for him, but worn to defuse the strife between them. Clothes that now caused guilt to shoot through him when he'd rather toss them. Clothes that caused unpleasant memories to surge when he wanted to forget.

Perrin ignored the box and pulled his ancient faded jeans—the one's Marge had threatened to throw away—off the hanger with a savage jerk. He slipped into them, found a pullover and shook out the wrinkles.

As Perrin headed for Rosita's, he plastered a fixed smile on his lips and hoped it would hide the unrest boiling inside.

~*~

"So you work on Saturdays?" The skinny young boy swayed as he maneuvered the game sticks, like a cornstalk blowing in a hard wind.

"Depends. I do a lot of catch up on paperwork when I'm behind. Check out a job now and then. Most times I shop, read, do wood projects, and get ready for tomorrow."

With an extra jab of the sticks, Blake gave up on the game. He turned. "What do you mean, get ready for tomorrow?"

"Sunday school. Tomorrow's Sunday."

"You go to Sunday school?"

"I teach."

"You teach Sunday school and go every Sunday."

Toni looked at the boy dressed in jeans with holes and a baggy sweatshirt, a look in his eyes she couldn't read. "Of course. Lots of people in Appleton go to Sunday school. We have special classes geared toward different age groups. It's a lot of fun. Would you like to go with me tomorrow?"

"Dad says it's an old fashion practice. People don't bother anymore." His gaze lifted to her eyes then shifted away. But not before she saw the moisture in them.

"Blake, what's wrong?"

"Nothing." His voice rose to an angry squeak.

Really? He didn't act like it was nothing. Had he had a bad experience, or had his parents forbidden him to go for some reason?

Her words were gentle. "If your dad doesn't mind, I'd love for you to go with me. We have two classes for your age group, and I'm sure you'll fit in one of them."

"I'll think about it." The words were nonchalant, but the eagerness in his eyes belied them.

"Just let me know if you decide to go."

With a studied casualness, he shrugged. "Sure."

"Good."

~*~

Perrin parked and walked inside the pizza pub. He caught sight of his son sitting at a booth, the friend opposite him. He strode toward them but the hot pink hat perched on the friend's head and the slender shoulders caught his gaze.

It wasn't Sid. Was Blake with a girl?

As he approached he heard a soft voice, the inflections rising and falling as it steadily spoke. The flow of the words was dramatic, and in spurts.

The friend was a girl all right. A girl reading. His twelve-and-a-half year old son was with a girl.

Perrin paused, listening. He caught the sound of his son's chuckle and the flap of a hand as the reader accompanied the words with a gesture. The ponytail of curls cascading out of the hat was shiny and dark, bouncing against her neck as she bobbed her head.

The voice seemed familiar, but he couldn't quite place it. Who was it?

Perrin stepped closer, and Blake looked up at him. The friend must have sensed his presence because her head turned at the same time. Happiness shone on Blake's face. The boy jumped up. "Dad."

Tension played on the friend's face as she shut her book.

With obvious wry recognition, he realized his presence presented no such thing as happiness for Toni DeLuca. But how did he expect her to react after his coldness last night?

He adjusted his own expression as he greeted his son, but his gaze lingered on Toni's dark eyes. Had she read the dismay following the surprise in his eyes?

She was flushed and tendrils of curls encircled her face, framing the heart of it. A smile touched her lips, but her eyes, big and luminous, held a hint of the wariness she obviously felt.

And the bruise on her cheek. She'd tried to cover it, but the darkness had bled through her attempts. Her eyes were huge and looked as if she'd been ill.

Had his actions last night given her that haunted look? No, he'd not caused the bruise. Then how on earth had she gotten it?

Toni jumped to her feet. "Well, hi again. Now that you're here, I'd better run. I've got to get ready for tomorrow and have a ton of things to finish up."

She bit her lip but before he could answer, Blake spoke up.

"What for? We're going to get something to eat. Come on, Toni, stay for pizza."

"Son, I'm sure Miss DeLuca has more important things to do than spend her noon with us...you." Did his voice sound as desperate as he felt?

Angry eyes—Toni's and Blake's—reproached him.

"Dad..."

"That's not true." Toni's words were clipped. "I would love to eat lunch with the charming Douglas family."

Was that sarcasm coming from between those red lips?

In spite of his sympathy minutes ago for her, Perrin narrowed his eyes.

"But..." She paused and tilted her head, her lips contemptuous.

His breath suspended, he wondered what was coming.

"...I want to give you guys your time together."

Relief swept over Perrin. Relief that she'd not attacked him, and relief that she'd not exposed his own rude behavior from the night before. He opened his mouth to speak, but Blake beat him to it.

"We don't care about that. We want you to join us, don't we, Dad?"

The boy turned toward his father, his tone pleading and his eyes calculating. "Dad?"

Perrin *didn't* want her with them. She was too dangerous to his emotions, and he was not to be trusted. He had to stay away from her. Couldn't she tell by his actions?

From the corner of his eyes, he could see Blake's gaze swing from Toni to him. At last the boy spoke, and his childish dignity pricked at Perrin's heart.

"I wanna have pizza with Toni, Dad. I invited her. Why can't we eat together?" The words were low and almost defiant, but disappointment laced its way through them.

Disappointment in him.

Hurt tugged at his emotions, but he shoved it away. How long had it been since *he*'d taken time for Blake?

Toni was protesting, but it was a background sound. Blake's words echoed in his ears and drowned her words. He could make excuses—Miss DeLuca wasn't on a book deadline. Miss DeLuca wasn't running from memories or from a past like his. Miss Deluca hadn't had a companion like he'd had.

But that didn't make up for neglecting his own flesh and blood.

Blake wasn't her son. Blake was his. The possessiveness shot through him and wrung the strength from him. He glanced again at Blake's challenging eyes and then turned to Toni, resolute. "I'd like for you to join us for pizza."

He was too formal, too stiff. As always. His jaw clenched. Why did he always come off sounding like a stuffy professor every time he was backed into a corner?

Because that's what he was.

Her beautiful eyes searched his, studied Blake a moment, and then she nodded and took a deep breath. "Okay. Pizza it is."

~*~

Trapped.

Trapped between Blake's need for her friendship and his father's antagonism and distrust against her. Truth be told, she was trapped between her own feelings. Drawn toward the man and fearful at what she might learn. Of being hurt.

If she'd read Perrin's eyes right and his actions correctly, at the beginning of last evening, he'd been interested.

And she'd responded to that admiration like a starved orphan.

Toni winced at her mental comparison. Was she that desperate for male attention?

Chapter Ten

Rosita's Pizzeria overflowed with customers. They'd had to wait forty-five minutes on their orders, but it'd been worth it. Perrin sat across from her and Blake, and she felt his gaze more than once. What was he thinking? Wishing?

"How about tossing the Frisbee after lunch?"

The excitement on Blake's face was well worth the time he'd given up writing.

"You mean it?"

"Of course. It's Saturday. We'll make a day of it." He looked at Toni. "Are you any good with a Frisbee?"

Toni felt a surge of recklessness spring through her. "Am I?"

Face screwed up in doubt, Blake jabbed, "Not as good as me."

"Ha. We'll see about that." Toni laughed and bumped him with her shoulder.

Blake's derisive snort exploded around them. "Yeah, right. Hey, there's a couple of guys I know. Okay if I go say hi?"

Perrin gave the room a quick glance, then shrugged. "I suppose so. Don't forget to come back."

Voices filled the air. Families talking. Friends laughing. Couples holding hands, snuggling close. Toni let her hands rest in her lap, the coziness of it all spreading through her. She seldom ate here, but it was a friendly, casual fast-food place that many in Appleton praised.

She turned back to Perrin and drew in a deep breath. Regardless of last night, or her bizarre running-from-him impulse this morning, she needed to show some semblance of friendliness. After all, he was a client.

"It is Perrin Douglas, isn't it? Did I remember the name correctly?"

The deep voice interrupted her planned attempt of reconciliation.

Perrin spoke first. "That's right. From last night. You're Rita Mae's friend. Sal, was it?"

The distinguished-looking older gentleman who'd sat beside Sylvia last night and at The Specialty House this morning.

"May I sit down for a moment?"

What were they to do? Say no? Toni nodded, and Perrin motioned toward Blake's spot beside Toni.

"Thanks." With a touch too much alacrity, the man sat and immediately propped his arm on the bench behind Toni.

Toni leaned forward and propped *her* arms on the table.

"I'm Salvadore, ma'am, but my friends call me Sal. Did I understand them right? You are Antonietta DeLuca?"

Ah, that explained the old-worldly atmosphere about him. His Spanish roots were showing, and Toni liked it. "I think I'm too young for you to call me ma'am." She smiled at him. "Yes, my name is DeLuca."

"I see." He tugged at his beard. "I won't keep you, but wanted to offer an invitation to a Christmas dinner I'm planning. I'm considering moving into the area and want to make the acquaintance of this charming town's best citizens."

"I'm not sure I qualify—"

"Oh, but I'm sure you do."

He interrupted, but it was so gallantly done, that Toni felt pleased at his genuine comment.

"Besides," he cocked his head at her in a teasing manner, "I've heard you run an excellent business. Who knows, I may need your services."

Laughing, she said, "I'm sure not everyone—"

Again he interrupted. "I may have heard one or two jealous remarks, but who minds them? Only the best have negative remarks made about themselves."

Toni eyed this man. What had given her the idea his eyes were too narrow? He was a perfect gentleman, gallant and handsome, and well-spoken too. When he took his leave, he didn't kiss her fingers, but his clasp said he'd like to.

~*~

"Wonder what he was up to?"

"I thought he was friendly."

"Sure you weren't suckered in by that fake accent and manners?" Perrin crossed his legs, angry that Toni was so oblique at seeing the man for what he was. "I met him last night and was not impressed."

Toni hesitated. She'd seen him last night from across the room. In spite of his distinguished looks, his eyes had alerted her that he was a man of which to be careful. So why now, had she suddenly been swept off her feet at his attention?

Was Perrin right to be cautious? Or was he jealous?

Of a sudden, Toni realized why she'd allowed herself to be caught up in the moment. Perrin's coldness last night. His reluctance this afternoon at her presence.

She was trying to make him jealous.

Eyeing him, she wondered if she'd succeeded.

~*~

"It's about time *you* called me Toni, isn't it?"

"I suppose so." His mouth widened in a sudden grin. "I'm a real conversationalist when I try."

And, magically, the tense atmosphere cleared.

"Hey, we all have those moments." Toni added.

"Why was your real name shortened to Toni?"

"When I was born, Daddy said that was much too long for such a little baby."

She smiled then sobered. Was that true and *had* he been there when she was born?

"Your mother...?"

"She died when I was a baby, I think."

"You think?"

Perrin's voice was as gentle as she'd ever heard it. Perhaps beneath that crusty exterior lurked emotions like love and sympathy. If only he would allow God to channel his negativity into something positive. If only she could help him. Big ifs.

"I can barely remember my mother."

"So you were close to your father?" Perrin's

face was serious, his eyes searching her own.

"Yes. Daddy and I did everything together. Picnics, the zoo, and school projects. He was my 4-H leader and my best cheerleader when I tried out for the lead part in the junior play. He went to every parent/teacher meeting. Insisted I go to college, although I didn't want to." She looked at Perrin, the tears stinging her eyes. "I loved him very much."

"And no man ever measured up."

"I dated a lot in high school and college. Thought once I'd found the man I wanted to spend my life with."

"I hear a but."

Toni shrugged. "After a summer away from each other, I realized I could live without him. That wasn't the kind of love I needed to feel for someone who would be with me for the rest of my life."

"No one since?"

This conversation was moving into the uncomfortable range. Enough talk about her. "What a boring topic. Tell me about yourself."

Perrin sat back in his seat. "I'm a history professor. Done a lot of ancestry work. I've traced my own ancestors back to the Revolutionary War."

"Impressive." Toni leaned forward, eager to hear more. "I wish I could say the same."

"I thought the Italians were abnormally family-conscious?"

"Very. But Daddy's grandparents immigrated, started a new life and kind of lost touch with the old family. Anyhow, he was always too busy to keep in touch. I think." Toni realized she knew very little about any extended family. Had her father saved photos of his family? Why hadn't she been more curious?

"Would you like me to do some work on it?"

The fear leaped in her throat. What if he found something she didn't want to hear, or worse, didn't want anyone, especially him, to know? "You'd have the time? I thought you were on some kind of deadline?"

"I am. It's my first fiction book, due at my editor's right after the first of the year. Gives me little time. I've got half the book to finish and the editing to do before I send the first draft on."

"What's your book about?"

A sheepish expression crossed his face. "My others were nonfiction historical topics. One ancestry book."

"And?"

He made a dismissive gesture with one hand. "But I've always had a secret desire to branch out into fiction. Decided the time was right."

She placed one hand on her side, cocked her head. "Are you going to tell me what it's about?"

His face grew red. "Adventure. Love. A lord turned pirate, bitter over some unjust division of lands. Ends up rescuing a lady when her family is killed."

"Ooh. Romance."

"I call it Romantic Adventure. I based it on some tales that's been passed down through my family."

"You had pirates in your family?"

"So I've been told."

His sudden grin sent her heart fluttering.

"Well, maybe one."

"That is so fascinating. I think it's great that you can write like that."

"Better wait till you read it before you pass on the admiration."

"I'd love to. Are you offering?" Toni was begging but didn't care.

"You really want to?"

"I'd love to read anything you wrote." Toni swallowed the words. Too mushy. Much too mushy. That warm, snuggly feeling was getting the best of her.

Heat suffused her face. She was as bad as his yo-yo attitude. What business did a construction business owner have flirting with a fiction-writing professor?

~*~

Toni stopped dead on the sidewalk in front of Rosita's. Even from here, she could tell something was wrong with her truck. It didn't sit right, leaning as if it was lopsided.

"What's wrong?"

She ignored Perrin's question and hurried forward. She didn't have time to reach it before a dark-dressed figure ran from behind it and headed down the street.

It looked like the same figure who'd been about to destroy their finished construction job days ago. The one who'd practically mowed her down. The one she'd suspected might be Perrin...

But if that was the case, then it couldn't have been...

Her gaze flashed to the man standing beside her.

Unless he had an accomplice.

Whew. Where had that crazy thought come from?

"Why *are* you here?"

His brow cocked up. "Here, as in Appleton? Or here, as at Rosita's Pizzeria?"

"Town. Both. I don't know."

"That makes sense."

He was laughing.

"Don't laugh at me. Why did you move here?"

"What business is it of yours why I'm here?"

"Because I *need* to know."

He studied her as if weighing her statement for believability. "To write and have quiet and forget."

That sounded innocent enough. Except for the 'forget' part. What was that about? This was the wrong way to go about everything. "I'm sorry. I'm a bit stressed out."

Perrin was walking around her truck. "Looks like someone slashed your two front tires."

Great. Time for a call for road service.

When she'd finished her call, Perrin asked, "Let us drop you off at home."

She considered his offer. There really wasn't a need to wait. Isaac knew her and knew her truck. He'd take care of it and let her know when it was drivable again. Sooner than her poor damaged Mustang, for sure.

She sighed and agreed as she climbed into his battered vehicle. "Thanks."

The ride went way too fast for her, and with a suggestion that reminded her of her impulsive friend, Caro Gibson, she said, "You can come in for a piece of apple pie, can't you?"

The two males didn't speak for a second or two, and Toni caught her breath. She shouldn't have asked. Perrin wasn't a friend. A business acquaintance, at best. A foe, at worst. What was she thinking? Of course, he had moved way down on her suspects list, not that she had many to consider. So what had been the reason for her harebrained invitation?

Who was she trying to fool? She didn't want the evening to end.

"Apple Pie?" The two male voices blended as one.

Perrin met Blake's eyes. "This woman knows how to tempt a man, doesn't she?"

"Dad, who was that goddess you told me about who was a temptress?" He slammed open the door as Perrin pulled into her drive and jumped out, ducking the teasing slap she aimed at him.

Toni laughed and shot the boy a mock-pout. "No homemade pie for ungrateful wretches."

For a moment, Blake stood rooted to the concrete sidewalk, staring down the street.

"What's wrong, Blake?" Toni passed him and heard him mumbling behind her.

Perrin cocked an eyebrow at her. "Have we mentioned women who bake real food gets our eternal thanks?"

"Shameless beggars." Toni flouted at him. She led the way to her front door. "Careful. Rod had to rig temporary steps for me."

Kicking her shoes to the side, she called back over her shoulder. "Those who eat have to work for it."

She smiled as the two followed her, almost

stumbling over their own feet.

"I'll begin the coffee. Blake, get the pie out of the pantry. Over there. Careful." She nodded the direction. "Perrin, there's milk for Blake in the fridge, and cream for our coffee. Mugs are in that cabinet."

Minutes later, Perrin slipped his first forkful of pie into his mouth. He closed his eyes, chewed, and swallowed then widened his eyes. "There's something wrong with this pie."

"What? What's wrong?" Toni took a hasty bite of her own slice. "It tastes okay to me." She glanced at Blake who grinned at her.

Suspicious, she turned back to Perrin.

"It tastes musty."

"Musty?"

"Yeah. Musty have some more."

Toni stared blankly for a minute before she took in Perrin's broad smile. She allowed her gaze to reach the ceiling as father and son slapped hands.

"You got her good with that one." Blake ribbed.

Toni sniffed. "A poor one, if you ask me."

"Can't take a joke, Miss DeLuca?"

She wrinkled her nose at him. "I like good ones."

Two slices later, Blake headed toward her bookcase and soon was absorbed in a book. Toni gathered plates and silverware and begin filling her dishwasher. Perrin stood and poured fresh coffee in their cups again.

"It's none of my business, but I couldn't help but notice that horrendous bruise on your cheek."

Toni straightened and wailed, "Does it look

that bad?" She must look like a monster.

"Not at all. I can't imagine how you got it. Wouldn't have anything to do with all that damage to your front porch, would it?"

Her gaze searched his face. Did he really not know? Had he been the attacker last night in the car? Her heart said no, but what did that organ know?

"Why do you drive that old station wagon around? You don't happen to own a big black car with a white stripe, do you?"

He blinked, and Toni narrowed her eyes at him. He was taking a bit too long to answer a simple question.

"No, I don't own a big black car with a white stripe. And I—I don't know why I keep the station wagon. Guess I never thought about it." He rubbed his hand over his hair. "No, that's not true. I think I do it because Marge—never mind. What does it matter?" For the first time that evening, he scowled at her.

And for whatever reason, his refusal to answer lifted her suspicion. His answer had been honest and heartfelt.

"Someone rammed me off the road here at my house last night, hence the bruise. My cheek hit the steering wheel."

That was real concern shining from his eyes. No faking that reaction.

When Toni sat down, Perrin indicated the pink notes lying on her countertop. "And the notes? They look like the one Manny gave you at the restaurant. Am I being presumptuous in asking what they're about?"

A wave of giddiness rolled through her. She'd forgotten all about them in her excitement at keeping her company longer. How could she let them lie out in plain sight? Now he'd be on his guard—if he was behind them.

"Probably." She gripped her mug, the heat stealing into her cold hands. She searched his face. "But that's okay. I suppose I might as well tell someone."

"First a wicked looking bruise, and now threats? They are, aren't they?" A frown creased between Perrin's eyebrows. "Doesn't sound good."

Her stomach rolled with nausea at the conflicting emotions stirring inside her. Was he behind the threats, and pushing to see what she knew?

Perrin gave her a quizzical look then nodded, his voice a quiet, calming effect on her stretched nerves. "I assumed you were getting threats at the restaurant. Your face gave you away. The slashed tires sealed my suspicion."

"Someone sent them addressed to me at work with no return address." Was that really her wobbly voice?

"Hmmm. You make very good coffee." He lifted his mug and sipped. "The person knows you. Think it could be from someone you've worked for?"

Toni shoved aside her mug and rubbed at her eyes. "I haven't a clue."

"No enemies? Anyone angry with you? Someone upset about something you've said or done? Maybe one of your jobs?"

"I can't think of a thing. And I have no enemies here in our town. It has to be a joke. Horrid, I know, but someone must think it funny."

"It's not a joke or they'd take credit for it eventually." Perrin's eyes reflected his far-away thoughts.

"I have no idea what they're talking about..."

"There has to be a reason. Someone doesn't love you." He drummed his fingers on the tabletop. "What have you done about it?"

Toni shrugged. "Ignored it. Called my pediatrician, but couldn't talk with him. Checked the statistics at the courthouse this morning. Thought maybe there might be some records of similar mischief that could lead me to a name or maybe of daddy being charged."

"Why your pediatrician?"

"Because he's one of oldest residents in town. If anyone knows anything about my family, it would be Dr. Felly." She grinned at the thought of the still-active man who'd been a part of her life forever. "I also did a small amount of Internet research. No luck. No news articles. Nothing that I could find."

"That's all good, but you don't know what you're looking for. You need to call the police. Let them find the person responsible."

"Absolutely not. I will not have my father's name dragged through small town mud-gossip."

Perrin tapped his fingers on the table top then leaned forward. "Don't mean to brag, but as I told you before I'm good at research. I've done enough, I should be. I'm not a detective, but if you'll trust me, I'll do some digging around. Bet we can, at least, find a clue as to who sent the note. And, at the most, find out if your father was involved in something less than honorable from his past."

"You want to help me find the person who sent those notes?"

He nodded and raised a hand when she started to speak. "I think my resources could be helpful. I know you don't want to consider your father as a criminal. But would you be satisfied to never know at this stage? Better accept my offer."

"Are you sure you want to do this?" Earlier, he'd given every indication of wishing her away from his presence. Was his aim to keep her close? Better to keep track of what she was learning? She could play that game too.

Why did he make her feel she was stumbling along on rough ground? Pulling her close with his smiles, shoving her away with his tart answers and cold dismissals?

"Of course, I'm sure. I have contacts. It won't be as hard as you think. Trust me."

Toni clenched the fingers resting on her lap into a fist and searched Perrin's face.

Could she?

Chapter Eleven

Trust me.

Ridiculous. He had no right to ask any woman to trust him. Now or any time.

Perrin paced up and down. Twenty steps to his window, twenty back to his desk. Fifteen to his door, fifteen back to his computer.

At last, he sat at his computer, typed in a command and watched the screen. Then he hammered out his request, hit send, and sat back, smiling. As good as he was, one of his past students, Turley Moore, was better. He would locate what he wanted. Perrin was confident he'd come through. Within days, if not hours, Turley would have the information about Toni's problem.

Perrin shut down his computer, stood, and stretched. It had been a good afternoon and evening. Fun. Interesting. Relaxing. He'd been a little too blatant in his anger. But that Sal man had come on to Toni like he owned her. Or wanted to.

What right did he have to object? He'd not given her any good reason to consider him as anything but a moody client.

The realization hit him. He wanted more. Deny his feelings all he wanted, that was the gist of it. No matter how he tried to keep away from Toni, he was being thrown into her presence. Blake's doing. Or his own weak desire to be with her.

He strode to their shared room—a temporary situation until the extra room was built on—opened the door and peered in. The lights were off and only a night-light lit the room. Enough to see his sleeping son.

Tonight on the way home from Toni's, Blake had told him he was going to Sunday school with Toni tomorrow. His voice shook with excitement.

Perrin frowned, scoffed. "Sunday school's for babies, don't you think?"

Blake did *not* think. His indignant tone told Perrin Toni had already filled Blake in. "No way. Toni's church has two classes for my age. It's a special ministry of their church. Even some adults have a Bible Study class for early Sunday mornings."

"Is this something you want to do? Toni hasn't twisted your arm?"

Blake slouched in his seat and crossed his arms. Perrin knew he was preparing for battle.

"As if someone could make me go if I didn't want to." Blake's gaze met his father's, his lips set in a mulish line, his shoulders stiff with determination, and the blue-green eyes radiating a challenge.

He'd made up his mind. Better back off and let him think he was agreeing. Blake would tire of the trial church experience quick enough.

"Fine. As long as that's what you want."

Perrin smiled to himself and changed the subject.

He reached down now and tugged the sheet over Blake's shoulder. How thin the boy was. Perrin remembered his own youthful build, the skinny frame and awkward limbs.

He'd outgrown some of that. He tried to visit the YMCA twice a week, but it was a chore when he'd rather be hammering out his story ideas.

Not much progress today on his book, but at least, he'd spent some time with Blake, even if he'd had to share him with Toni DeLuca.

The phone rang.

The alarm clock read eleven twenty-seven.

Toni Deluca's voice lilted when he lifted the receiver. "Hope it's not too late. Wanted to invite you for lunch tomorrow after church."

"I was headed to bed." The rebuke in his voice would have discouraged all but the bravest, and he gritted his teeth in agitation. Too strong. Too strong. What was it with him? Every time he turned around she was there, gaze fastened on him, sweet smile coaxing from him what she wanted. And he rebuffed her every time.

Unlike the suave Sal, he wasn't strong enough to admit and go after what he wanted. And all because one woman had betrayed his trust.

"Oh, I'm sorry." She was abashed, at his rudeness, no doubt. The hurt oozed through the line as thick as a storm cloud dripping rain.

He groaned.

"I'm preparing a roast and applesauce cake." She puffed out a little breath. "I can't eat it all myself."

Perrin imagined the browned roast, tender and succulent from its own juices, surrounded by quartered chunks of potatoes, carrots and onions. His mouth watered with sudden appetite. He hadn't had roast since before moving here, and that had been the restaurant variety.

Maybe he needed to rethink the refusal hovering on his tongue.

~*~

Toni gripped the phone receiver tighter. It'd taken all her courage to call the Douglas home this late. As usual, he'd sent her to the low end of a yo-yo string with his terse reply.

She'd heard his refusal coming and hurried to lay out her menu. Wasn't the old saying 'the way to a man's heart was through his stomach' true anymore?

Not that she was trying to get anywhere near his heart. But after all, she did like a little company now and then.

"I've invited a few friends for Sunday dinner after the service tomorrow." Why had she told him that? Now he'd know it would be eaten and not wasted.

"Please say yes. I really would like it if you and Blake could come." Goodness, that was laying it on pretty thick. Why should he care what she liked?

She heard him take a breath.

Hear it comes.

"What time do you want us?"

Toni sank to her bed, knees weak.

Only after she set the phone on its stand did she realize she'd forgotten her plan to invite him to the morning service. How could she have forgotten?

She closed her eyes, lay back against the headboard, then pulled her purse up beside her. Without looking, she dug inside and pulled out the piece of paper Manny gave her at Apple Blossoms Friday night. The one she'd refused to think about. As if she could forget. Opening her eyes, she unfolded the paper and read the words again.

You don't believe me? I have the proof. You are adopted. Meet me Sunday night, 9:30, at 727 Beechnut Road. DON'T bring anyone. In case you think to involve the police, I'll make sure someone you care about suffers for it. Come alone. You'll have the proof then.

Toni felt the blood draining from her face just as it had at the restaurant.

~*~

Toni stood by her classroom door the next morning, greeting her usual pupils. She spoke a special warm welcome to two new girls, but kept a keen eye out for Blake.

She'd offered to pick him up since this would be his first visit, but he'd insisted he wanted to walk. The last straggling pupil entered, and sure he wasn't going to show up, she started to close the door. Her eye caught his figure walking toward her, down the long hallway, hesitant and shy.

She reached for his hand, squeezed it, and ushered him in the room.

Although she made eye contact with all of her class, Toni's heart leaped with joy when she realized Blake kept his gaze on her through the whole lesson. He asked no questions, yet Toni noticed he listened attentively to all the other questions buzzing around him.

She bid each youth a friendly good-bye at

the close of the class and stepped into the hallway.

Blake waited, leaning against a wall, one athletic-clad foot scuffing a toe on the tiled surface.

"Can I stay for the service? You think it'd be okay?"

"That's wonderful." Toni enthused.

"Dad said he'd meet me at your house at one."

"That's wonderful, too."

~*~

Dismay filled him when Perrin Douglas arrived at Toni's home and saw the four vehicles parked in her driveway. He hadn't moved here to begin another social round. Why had he allowed himself to be tempted with some homemade cooking?

Toni welcomed him with a warm smile, her eyes flicking gold specks at him as she drew him into the house. He sought and found Blake who sat in a corner talking with a tall girl, freckles covering her nose and brown hair framing her long oval face.

Toni linked her arm in Perrin's as she led him around the room. "You met Starli and Manny at the restaurant."

Starli greeted him coolly, but the older man stood and shook hands, his voice friendly. "Good to meet you again."

"And this is my other oldest and dearest friend and the imp of the town, Caroline Gibson, better known as Caro. She co-owns Undiscovered Treasures."

The dark blond bounced out of her chair, ignored his extended hand, and gave him an impulsive hug. "Wow, I'm really glad to know a professor as a friend instead of a teacher."

He couldn't help himself. Perrin laughed.

"And this is Stanley Robinson, our youth pastor." Toni turned to the stocky man. "He's batching it this week while his wife is at her parents."

Toni smiled and nodded at the man on the other side of Caro. "Toby Gibson is the other owner of Undiscovered Treasures, although he limits his duties to traveling and collecting the treasures they sell."

When Toni excused herself and started to leave, Perrin stopped her. "Want some help?"

"Sure you don't want to visit?" Toni glanced at her friends, then back at him.

"I'm sure." Anything to keep from being stranded in a room full of strangers.

"Caro and Starli usually help, but I see they're involved in their conversations."

As Toni dished up her roast beef and vegetables, Perrin poured the drinks, set relish trays, and individual plates of salads on the table.

Fifteen minutes later, the group settled at Toni's huge dining table and clasped hands while the youth pastor offered a simple prayer of thanksgiving.

Perrin shot a look at the raven-haired beauty sitting beside him and swallowed. He hadn't forgotten. She was still as lovely as he'd thought.

His eyes flicked to her two friends. He smiled as his gaze lighted on Caroline Gibson and felt at once at home with her personality. Her homely face beamed with enthusiasm as she waved the fork she held in her hand. He imagined whatever that girl tackled she did it with all her being.

His gaze shifted. Starli, a true beauty, would rate as well as any contestant in a pageant. Unlike Caroline's messy do, not a silver-blond hair strayed out of place. Her creamy smooth face was a composed model of supposed serenity, every one of her movements calculated.

As her gaze lifted to his own, her green eyes held more than a hint of coolness in them. Her chin tilted ever so slightly, and he knew his opinion hadn't changed. She was one of those carved ice figurines. Lovely to look at, cold to the touch.

"What do you think?" Toni's question on his left came at him in a whisper.

"Meaning?" He lowered his voice to match her own and indicated the food on his plate. "You're a good cook. This is delicious."

Toni laughed. "Thanks. But I meant my friends. Do you like them?"

Perrin hedged and kept his voice lowered. "Don't put me on the spot."

"If you're talking about Starli, I told you a little of her history. She'll warm up when she learns you can be trusted."

Trusted. Perrin frowned. Great word choice to describe him.

Caro's saucy voice interrupted his thoughts. "Perrin, I need your help over here. Stan and Toby are ganging up on me. Help."

Her pert, freckled nose wrinkled in disgust. She stretched out a hand in mock despair and demanded his attention.

Perrin shoved at his glasses and grinned at the girl. "What's the problem?"

"Toby thinks we should start selling a local artist's paintings, and they are so-o-o gross. And Stan, who's usually level headed, is agreeing with him." She propped a hand on her trim waist. "How's that for friendship? Forget brothers. And I guess I'll have to add certain youth pastors to my list of forgettable people."

The group howled at her grievances.

"I understand." Perrin did understand. Some of his dearest friends had betrayed him, and that wasn't easily forgotten or forgiven. "Those who are the closest to us are often the least to be trusted."

For a second no one said anything. Gazes from around the table fastened on him and as quickly dropped. Nervous laughter sprang from first one set of lips, then another.

Caro clapped her hands, and her mouth widened in a teasing grin as though obvious to the strain his words had bred a second ago. "A man after my own heart. From now on, I'll use my own judgment."

A stab of guilt shot through Perrin at his own levity. How could he joke about trust when he'd failed so miserably in his own life?

Stan ladled another spoonful of carrots onto his plate. "There's not a thing wrong with Andy's work. It has feeling."

"Yeah, right." Caro drew her lips down in a pout. "Depressing work. Makes me so lonesome I cry every time I see it."

"I'm so l-o-n-e-s-o-m-e..." Stan crooned, laughing.

"Come on, Caro, quit being so dramatic.

Just because you love sunshine doesn't mean everyone else wants 24 hours of it." Toby nodded at his sister and mocked, "She needs to move south."

As the brother and sister erupted into a good-natured argument, Stan cleared his throat. "The Festival is coming up soon. I know I can count on your support."

Choruses of assurance echoed around the room.

"What can we do to help?" Caro waved a hand at her brother to shush him.

"We've got all the volunteers needed for now. Just be there to support our booth."

"Let's go together. Make a caravan." Caro crowed. "Decorate our vehicles with signs about the church."

"Whoa," Stan laughed. "I can't do that. I'm an early bird that day. Have to be there to set up the booth at six."

"Neither can I." Toni smiled at her friend. "Though it's a great idea."

"Ergh. I guess I'll have to go with Toby." Caro frowned at her brother.

"And don't forget, muddlehead," Toby reached over to ruffle his sister's hair. "I promised to help Andy set up his own booth of paintings. I have to be early too. If you're riding with me, you're going to have to get out of bed before noon."

Toni joined in laughing at Caro's disgruntled expression.

"You're not going?" Perrin asked in a low voice.

"I am, but I'm well used to my very precious friend's ideas. I'm not waiting till afternoon to get to the festival." She slid a small bite of asparagus into her mouth, chewed, and swallowed. "Would you like to go?"

"Is this an event that I need to attend to enhance my education?"

"Definitely." Toni smiled and stabbed at a carrot.

"If you'll go as my partner, then I'm game."

"Love to." She rose to refill the pot roast platter. When she returned, she said to Perrin, "We'll probably walk downtown after dinner and look at all the Christmas decorations." Wisps of her dark hair curled around her ears and touched her neck.

"Is this an every Sunday event?"

"Oh, yes." Toni nodded at her friends. "Most times when they eat here, we walk downtown, through the apple orchard behind my home or even around the Indian ruins."

Her face glowed. "But wandering around in the orchard is my favorite. Those knobby old trees have lost their leaves by now. They'll be covered in snow soon. Like little dwarf people."

"The way I'm eating, I'll need some exercise." For just a second he'd been tempted to express his interest. The trouble was, he really was looking forward to the whole afternoon with her. But not yet. He couldn't let her know it yet.

When he looked up, Starli's untrusting gaze met his.

Chapter Twelve

Toni lifted her head, her eyes on the sky. She drew in a long breath of the nippy air, held it and let it out, then hugged her bulky sweater tightly around her body.

Up ahead, Blake and Britney—Stan's daughter—were laughing wildly. She grinned at their unrestrained happiness. Blake was such a dear. Britney would be a good friend to him. Bring him out of his shyness. She was glad she'd thought about inviting someone his age to dinner.

Toni turned to look at Perrin and found him staring at her. She felt the heat rise to her cheeks.

"Beautiful."

A rush of happiness tingled its way through her. She was being ridiculous. Giddy as a teenager over a compliment. Reckless in taking anything this man said too deeply.

"I wasn't talking about the scenery."

"I know." She let out a sigh of pleasure and held out her arms. "I love living in Appleton. Everyone knows everyone, and yes, sometimes some are too nosy, but we're also helpful and caring and look out for each other."

"A true country attitude."

"That's right."

"Tell me about your orchard. Why didn't we walk there today?"

Toni shrugged. "Almost Christmas. The call of Christmas and the decorations lure us downtown."

"Go on."

"But I can't wait till the trees are in full bloom again which is my favorite time of year, *and* apple blossoms are my favorite flowers."

"I thought fall and winter was your favorite so you could use the fireplace you love."

"It's my *almost* number one favorite." She laughed. "I love it when the trees bud and bloom too. Absolutely divine."

"I don't think I'd be guessing wrong to assume apples are your favorite fruit."

Toni's grin widened. "Did you like my cake? I added a touch of vanilla flavoring to it."

"Don't remind me." Perrin groaned. "I ate two pieces. I won't be eating for a week after this afternoon."

"Sure. I believe that." Toni scorned his answer.

"What else do you enjoy besides the seasons? And carpentry and old cars." His eyes twinkled at her behind the lens of his glasses.

Toni admired the way the bright sunlight brought out the blue in his eyes. The same blue as the checked shirt beneath his jacket. His hands were shoved deep within his pants pockets, his hair waved ever so slightly in the light breeze.

The way he matched her stride pleased her too, not so fast she had to run to keep up, but neither too slow that she constantly had to stop to wait on him. She slowed her own speed to touch the lamp post, its early evening glow shedding a warmth that over shadowed the increasing crispness in the air.

She closed her eyes and imagined the scent from the tiny buds in the spring seeping out. "I love soft romantic music, the old buildings in town, and good books."

She tilted her head, questioning him if he'd heard enough. At his nod, she went on, abandoning herself to expressing what she seldom said.

"I love misty mornings, our rolling hills, and the hay bales left in the fields. I love our apple orchards. Strolling in them is romance personified. Watching the trees go from bare brown branches reaching to the sky to green leafy boughs hanging low to the earth full of ready-to-be-harvested apples is exciting to me." She swung round to him and laughed.

"You feel intensely."

Toni struggled to bring her emotions under rein. What on earth was she doing? Why had she let herself go like that? She hardly knew the man and worse, a few days ago, she thought him trouble.

She grimaced. "It's the Italian in me. Dad was very expressive and taught me to be the same. He always said there was no shame in feeling, only in being afraid to feel."

"He was right. You have beautiful thoughts and a lovely way of expressing them. If only I had half that talent in my writing."

Toni let go of the post that threatened to cling to her chilled fingers. "Thanks. As I've said before, I love my life and enjoy all of it, for the most part."

Her eyes sought out Starli who stood with Stan, listening with bent head as he talked. "I suppose most people would say I've had an easy life. No worries, a loving father, good friends."

"Some might even say you've been handed life on a silver tray." Perrin said and leaned against the gazebo they stood beside.

"Perhaps I did. I know I grew up with no cares. Thought I had the best daddy in the whole world. Anything I wanted, I got." She wrinkled her nose. "Within reason, of course."

"Of course. Sounds as if you were spoiled."

"I probably was."

"Actually, you haven't turned out too badly."

Toni laughed, pleased his face had shed the reserve and sadness. He'd slipped his normal burden from his shoulders, whether consciously or unconsciously.

She lifted her hands, cupped her mouth and called out to her friends. "We're heading back. Anyone want tea and cookies?"

"So you're starting work on my home Monday?"

"Yes. You really do need to consider doing more elaborate work on it." As they retraced their steps, Toni explained her meaning. "Your house could be outstanding. It looks as if someone started out with Tudor plans, years ago, then ran out of money."

"You mean I was duped by the realtor when I bought it?"

Toni touched his arm with two fingers. "I doubt it. They were asking a fair price for the neglected state of it. Not having the experience in dealing with houses and things like that, you didn't realize what all needed done to bring it up to livable conditions. The house isn't bad looking. But with more additions and some inside work, it'd be stunning."

Perrin rubbed a hand across his chin. "That's a thought. I like the location and the basic house plan, but it'd be nice to have more room."

"The addition you're adding will help some." She ran up her back steps then turned to look down at him, "I've some apple fritters. But, of course, if you're so full, you won't want any."

Perrin stopped, one foot on the first step, and scratched his ear. "You know what, I think I've worked up an appetite, with all that walking we did."

Toni laughed and flouted over her shoulder as she entered her kitchen. "That was nothing. We didn't even explore the orchard or the ruins and caves. We barely got started."

Perrin followed her and held up a hand. "Whoa. I have a book to finish. I don't have time to loaf like some people."

Toni shrugged out of her sweater and tossed it onto a chair.

Yeah. You know more about me than I've learned about you. Why does every conversation we have work its way back to me? Why can't I get anything personal out of you?

The cups she wanted to use were in a high cabinet, and she stretched to reach them then set nine of them on her countertop. She adjusted a burner on her stove before lifting her gaze to meet Perrin's. His wide grin shooed away her doubts.

Who cared what she knew? Right now, it was enough to be here, in her kitchen, with this fascinating man.

Toni smiled back, but felt it draining away when she caught the image of a tall figure standing in the doorway. "Rod? Is something wrong? Roxie's okay?"

The man reached out and pulled her into the circle of his arm, guiding her into the hallway. "Yeah, she's fine." He drew in a deep breath. "But I do have bad news."

She gripped his arm with both hands. "Tell me quick."

"Someone's stolen the material we had loaded ready to go in the morning to the Douglas job."

"No. I wanted to get the work perfect for him." Another job disrupted. Had someone slugged her in the stomach? Toni jerked her head toward the kitchen. "What will he say?"

"It'll set us back a few days waiting on a replacement. But I think we can work some long days to catch up. It's the money I'm worried about. You gonna be okay with this now?"

Toni wanted to groan. Instead she laid her forehead on Rod's broad arm.

"Buck up, missy. I wouldn't have told you—"

"No. I needed to know." Toni lifted her head and pulled away. "Did you call the police?"

At his nod, she said, "Good. First thing in the morning, put in our order for that replacement. If we're careful, maybe we'll only lose a couple days."

"Right. You've got it."

"One other thing, Rod." As Toni pulled the notes out of her pocket, she rattled off the threats she'd received. "Now this last one's asking me to meet them at Perrin Douglas's house tonight."

"Why his home? Absolutely not." Rod crossed his arms as if he couldn't be budged.

"I've got to do this, Rod. I'm telling you because I need to know someone has my back."

Rod studied her for a long minute then growled. "I suppose you're right. But I'm going to be posted early enough to watch for who shows up and when Douglas leaves. And I'm giving Eddie a head's up. He might seem a cookie short of a baker's dozen, but he's a good egg to have on your side." He glared at her as if daring her to refuse his conditions.

"Okay. That makes sense."

"Not a word to Douglas, hear me?" He eyed her, knowingly.

Heat rushed to her cheeks. Were her feelings that obvious? "Not a word. Thanks, Rod."

When Rod left, Toni took a few minutes to lean against the wall. What next? She had no idea, but prayed that Perrin would never find out she'd messed up yet again.

~*~

Toni turned onto Beechmont Street and approached Perrin's house slowly. His old jeep wasn't in the driveway and the house was dark. Was he really gone? If it was him, he may have thought sending her here would point her suspicions in a new direction. If it wasn't him, who was trying to get her to think it was?

It made no sense. Nothing did. Either Perrin was innocent and ignorant of all this or an actor made for Hollywood.

And if he wasn't involved—wasn't home

even—who was here waiting for her?

Every instinct urged her to go home and ignore the note. But the threat to someone close to her scared her. If they were sincere enough to try to scare her and to destroy her company jobs, then she wouldn't put it past them to hurt her friends.

Toni opened the truck door, her gaze darting from bush to tree, scanning the porch, studying each window in the front.

Nothing. No sign of anyone. Was Rod here? And Eddie?

A hoax?

She'd never know if she didn't walk up those steps and knock on the door. Every fiber in her body screamed at her to not be stupid. But surely they wouldn't hurt her. Embarrass, harass, even ruin her business, but not harm her in any serious physical way. A few notes and site destructions seemed mild treatment for someone bent on killing her. On the other hand, the car accident was pretty serious. And Shawn's accident wasn't anything to sneeze at either.

Perrin seemed a logical suspect to point a finger at; friendly and anxious to help, withdrawn and sarcastic the next. He might be suffering from some past injury but that didn't excuse his extreme behavior.

Or, it didn't in her eyes.

She lifted her hand and knocked.

There was no way she'd break into the Douglas house. No matter what the note said. She should have gotten permission from Perrin to wait inside, but it would have involved a detailed explanation, one she wasn't ready to give. Rod had ordered not a word to Perrin, and she agreed.

Besides, what if he was the perpetrator of her troubles?

Backing up, she descended the steps and her gaze took in the porch, or at least, as much of the wraparound as she could see. No one lurked with obvious intentions of pouncing on her.

The night was quiet. Stars twinkled merrily in the heaven above. A few clouds scooted lazily from west to east, obscuring the full moon, then scampered on, leaving the night lit with a blue-black dimness.

Toni dragged in a deep breath. It was now or never. Tiptoeing up the steps again, she cringed when one step creaked in protest. If the note-sender skulked close by, he now knew she was here.

The old-fashion swing swayed a little, beckoning. Well, it was as good a place as any to wait for the information he'd promised. She settled into the swing, listened and relaxed. With a gentle shove of her foot, she set the swing in motion.

The touch on her shoulder sent her almost jumping to her feet, but the pressure increased and held her in place.

An obviously faked deep voice growled behind her back. "Don't turn your head."

It didn't sound like Perrin, but who could tell with the bad imitation?

"What do you want?"

A harsh laugh. "I want you to admit to the town about your birth."

That again. "But why? What will it

accomplish?"

"Not so fast. You'll learn more if you play the game the way you're told." The hand slid off her shoulder. The person behind her moved. "Here. Read it when you get home."

Toni looked down at the paper drifting downward in the light breeze to her lap. "What is this?"

No answer.

"I still don't understand."

A taunting laugh from the tree at the edge of the property slithered toward her. Toni glanced at the figure—small and thin—who lifted a hand at her.

She bounded from the swing, sending it rocking crazily on its chains, and saw two tall figures appear from two different hiding places. But even as she ran down the steps, she knew she wouldn't catch the first person.

Turning his back, he ran down the sidewalk and around the distant corner, his laugh floating behind like the tail on a kid's kite.

Rod ran back to her while the policeman ran on down the street after the illusive, laughing figure.

"Are you all right?"

She nodded and handed Rod the paper.

Rod glanced through it, bushy eyebrows lifted. "What kind of craziness is this? You're adopted? Makes no sense."

"I know." Toni bit her lip. "But it's my birth certificate. They don't lie."

Head still shaking in denial, Rod stared down at the paper.

Confusion gnawed at her inner being. Like the smiley face card, the wave from this person radiated kid-ish actions. Yet would a kid, even a teen, hatch an elaborate scheme such as going on in her life? But the body size—smaller and slimmer. Definitely not an adult. Not Perrin.

But his son?

That was laughable. A grown man using his son to terrorize her? And why? Why would Perrin want to scare her, ruin her business?

His company the last few days had been—wonderful. No way any man could make such a turnabout from one day to the next. A Dr. Jekyll/Mr. Hyde person? She didn't think so.

Could he be working for someone else?

Ridiculous. A history professor sans criminal.

No. She couldn't accept it.

Truth was, she didn't want to.

Chapter Thirteen

The sound of a singing, shower-muted, off-key voice woke Perrin Monday morning. Blake. Why was he up so early? He lay in his bed and listened to his son's lusty lungs belting out the tune.

Ten minutes later as he dropped back off to sleep, a tentative voice whispered his name, and the mattress dipped beside him.

"Are you awake, Dad?"

Perrin rolled over. "Why are you up so early?" He squinted at the clock on his bedside table.

"Toni's beginning our addition today. I wanted to be up and ready for them when they get here."

"I don't think they'll be here at six-thirty in the morning."

"Seven-thirty. I asked her what time, and she said Rod and the crew would be here then to begin digging the foundation. I don't want to miss watching any of it." The lopsided grin plastered on his face drew his lips up into a Howdy-Doody grin. "Besides, I'm hungry. Want me to fix you something?"

Perrin started to shake his head then saw the hopeful look on Blake's face. "Okay. What are you making?"

"Pancakes?"

"Sounds good. Need any help?"

Blake bounced up. "Nope. I mean, no. Go ahead and get ready. Can I use the package of bacon?"

They were still eating when a caravan of vehicles pulled up in their driveway. Blake jumped up and headed to the back door. "They're here."

"Hey. What about cleaning up?"

The boy stopped. "I cooked, you clean. Fair division of labor."

"I'll remember that." Perrin waved a hand at him and glanced at the clock. "Go. Don't get in their way. You have exactly 40 minutes before you have to head to school."

He half expected to see Toni in the group, but when he peered out the kitchen window, Rod and his four helpers were the only ones in sight. He stood watching as they unloaded some kind of machinery, then turned back to his computer.

It looked like Toni would hold true to her word and leave the manual labor to Rod and his crew. He allowed himself a satisfied sigh.

He spent all morning at his computer, the sounds of an engine, background noise to his typing, playing in his ears. By the time he took a break at noon, he felt satisfied at the progress he'd made. Another chapter done. If he could keep this up, he'd meet his deadline with time to spare.

After he'd eaten some of the roast beef Toni had sent home with him and Blake, Perrin prepared a sandwich for Blake then placed it on the top shelf in the fridge where his son would find it. He grabbed a bottle of water and headed back to his study.

Sitting at his desk, he checked his email and read the message from Turley. Nothing conclusive yet on the research for Toni, but he had some inside—as he called it—sources that he would check with today or tomorrow. Wednesday, or Thursday at the latest, should give them something.

Maybe he'd have good news to tell Toni soon.

~*~

It was all Toni could do to keep from going to the Douglas work site, but when the phone rang, and it was Eddie Snider, Toni focused on what the man had to say.

"Got a hit on the man you asked about, Miss Toni."

"Tell me."

"He's been arrested in a couple different states for scamming and misdemeanors. Nothing serious, but sure as anything annoying. Trouble is, he's a right skillful and shady character, able to assume different personalities when it pleases him."

"Our Kevin?" How could she and Rod been so deceived?

"Yep. Same guy. I'd be getting rid of him, unless, of course, you want to let me in on what's going on. Then I'll be glad to slip around and hook some handcuffs on him."

"I don't have anything concrete yet, Eddie. But I'll give you a yell when I do."

"You be careful, Miss Toni. Don't you be doing anything your daddy wouldn't have liked."

"Yes, sir."

Shawn had known what he was warning her

about. She'd have to give Rod the news so he could keep his eye on the man.

Toni hit an all-time record in sorting the stack of mail Roxie dumped on her desk. She dragged herself through the financial books, recording, double-checking and adjusting. When she caught herself glancing at her big wall clock for the nth time, she shoved away from her desk. It was almost four.

A quick drive-by would settle her nerves and shouldn't hurt anything. If she could get past Roxie.

Roxie's raised eyebrow greeted her, and a suspicious gaze drilled into her. "Where do you think you're going?"

"Out."

"Yeah, right." Roxie's country twang had never been more pronounced. "You're going out to the Douglas's home."

Toni straightened, tugged at the cap restraining her curls, and refused to face her office manager.

"You already know Mr. Douglas is antsy about women. Why do you want to go out there and chance agitating him more?"

"Don't scold, Roxie dear. I'm not going to interfere with your precious Rod's work. I just want to make sure everything's going as planned. Besides, Perrin seems to have changed his attitude toward me. I think he likes me."

Roxie lowered her head, preparing for battle. "What makes this job more important than all the others Rod has no problem handling?"

"Roxie, I'm just going to drive by. You know Rod won't care if I'm there or not." Toni winked at her.

Roxie sniffed. "Of course, he won't. He worships the ground you walk on."

"And you don't?"

Roxie shot her a don't-push-your-luck look. "The trouble with you, Toni DeLuca, is you're spoiled. That's the plain and simple truth of it."

Toni laughed and let the door slam behind her.

With both windows rolled down in the truck, the nippy wind whipped into her face. She pulled up to the curb of the Douglas house and wished she'd thought to stop for a sandwich. Her grumbling stomach told her it was past time for lunch.

Rod perched on the seat of the backhoe and ably maneuvered the machinery about the yard. His three helpers gestured, wielded shovels and strung string. Her eyes caught sight of a skinny figure looming close by. His head swiveled back and forth, his gaze never leaving the action spinning around him.

Toni smiled as she shoved open her truck door, and was half way across the ground before two of the workers and Blake saw her. She waved.

Blake trotted up to her. "Wow, this is so awesome. I didn't know so much work goes into building a room."

"All the questions he's been asking, won't be long till he can take charge." Rod's voice interrupted them. The tall man strolled up, and Toni realized he'd turned the machine off. He lifted a grimy hand and wiped at the sweat glistening on his forehead. "What are you doing here? Is something wrong?"

The heat crept up her neck. "Well…"

Rod's eyes narrowed. "I get it."

"What?" Blake looked from one to the other, then his gaze returned to the crew still working. "Hey, what are they doing now?" He loped across the yard.

Rod shook his head. "That boy must have gotten up before the sun cracked the horizon, cause he met us when we pulled in. He hung over our shoulders this morning, and now he's at it again with a million questions. I've had to warn him twice already to stay back from the equipment."

"Does he listen?"

"You know kids." Rod shrugged. "We should pour the footer in the early morning. A couple days from now we'll start the block. Can you tell me again why Douglas wanted a mini basement?"

"Said he wanted it for Blake. Sort of a clubhouse thing. He's into geology and science projects so figured it would be a better place than the kitchen or his own room."

"Gotcha. Makes sense."

Toni questioned him with her eyes.

"Haven't seen him. Don't know what he's been doing all morning." Rod's gaze roamed over the construction site.

"He's a writer and trying to beat a deadline."

"Is that right?" Rod cast another look at the big house, respect in his eyes. "Since you're here, you might as well come over and see what we've done. I think we're making good progress considering the theft last week."

"Great." Toni picked her way past the mounds of dirt. "The guys who wanted the dirt will be by to get the extra?"

"Course. They'll pick up any we don't plan to use before we leave today."

Toni flashed a smile at her supervisor. "On top as usual."

"Only way to be."

She walked around the site with Rod, double-checking their plans.

Rod excused himself, climbed back onto the backhoe and started it. With a careful glance around, he swung the arm in an arch.

As if time was gripped by a giant hand, it slowed and unfolded in turtle-creeping fashion. The swinging arm. The boy running up to the edge of the hole. A worker's yell of warning. The boy's flailing arms as the arm slammed into him, and he fell backward.

Toni stood horrified as she watched it all happen, unable to scream and surely unable to do a thing to stop it. In the background, she heard a door slam and saw the running figures.

Somewhere in that minute, Rod shut off the equipment, the quiet so loud she crossed her arms in horror.

Rod jumped off the hoe, and his feet had barely touched the ground before he'd leaped into the hole.

Her heart fluttered faster as she saw Perrin stop at the edge of the hole, glance at her, then jump into the hole after Rod.

Had her heart stopped beating? That look Perrin had shot her. The anguish in his eyes was her undoing. He would, of course, blame her. And, likewise, she'd never forgive herself if Blake was hurt.

Fortunately, someone was thinking quicker than her. As she fumbled for her cell, she realized one of her workers was already speaking into his, giving the directions to the person on the other end, for emergency help.

Rod had shed his flannel jacket and laid it over the boy. Toni wanted to slide down to them, but that look from Perrin stopped her. She'd promised him she'd stay away, and he would make sure she took the blame for Blake's distraction. Her supervisor. Her employees. Her presence.

It was her doing.

Within minutes, the ambulance people had the boy—protesting—on a stretcher and ready to load. When Perrin strode toward her, Toni bit her lip and tried to brace her trembling limbs.

"Why are you here?" The distrust in his voice spun her heart straight to her feet. His eyes shown like blue ice.

Toni caught her breath, her spirits sinking. "I...I..."

"You said you always left the work up to your guys."

"No, I didn't say that exactly. I said I leave the labor up to my men. That doesn't mean I don't stop by to check on the progress, to make sure all is as we planned. I stopped by today to make sure everything's going the way you want."

"And see what happened. I knew last night I should have stayed away from you."

She'd expected to get the blame, but she hadn't known how much it would hurt.

Why hadn't she stayed away? If only she'd

listened to Roxie.

His accusing gaze darted back to her. "You couldn't resist, could you? Women do that, you know. Keep everything in an uproar. Did you come to let everyone know you've thought of something more brilliant than our original plans?"

It wouldn't have hurt any more if he'd stuck a knife between her ribs. Only it wasn't a rib bleeding, it was her heart. Bleeding out hope and joy and belief. Hope that they could be friends, joy that yesterday had brought, belief that something good would come of her effort to be his friend.

She fought back the tears, her voice stiff from the strain. "I thought we were friends."

"Friends? I don't trust you. You can't trust me. We're in business, far from friendship."

You can't trust me. The words rang with special meaning. "That's not—"

Again Perrin interrupted her. "You almost had me fooled. I was beginning to think you were different, but you're just like the rest. Determined to have your way, regardless of the cost."

Toni stiffened, the Italian in her suddenly angry at the unjust accusation and determined to make him understand. "That's *not* true—"

But Perrin held up a hand and plowed over her indignant words. "I really don't care what you think or want or say. Just don't think you can come here and tell the Douglas family what to do. We're not interested." His shrug conveyed his message even without the harsh words.

"Why don't you let your supervisor,

whatever his name is, do his job? And you do yours, whatever that is. And stay out of my life."

With that, he turned his back and climbed into the EMS vehicle, the door slamming behind him.

Toni stood rooted. The angry heat seeped from her body, letting the icy cold settle around her heart. Her gaze remained fixed on the ambulance as it moved out of the drive, siren blaring. The sound was such a final one, it kept her rooted to the spot long after the vehicle had vanished from sight.

Rod was moving toward her, but she was down the side walk and headed toward her truck.

From the corner of her eyes, she saw him stop and study her, but she didn't slow her pace. Climbing into her truck, she was tempted to lay her head on the steering wheel and allow her feelings free rein. Allow the tears hidden beneath the surface to course down her cheeks.

She wanted to argue with the obstinate man who judged all women by someone who'd obviously hurt him very much. She wanted to weep at the foolish words he'd spat out and the barrier he'd erected with no thought of how it would ever be torn down.

~*~

Perrin sat beside the cot his son lay on. Already he regretted his anger. When he'd seen Blake fall into that hole, the terror that had enveloped him tore away the blanket of indifference he'd used to hide the hurt his wife's betrayal had done. Yet the awful, unjust words he'd just hurled at Toni left a bitter taste in his mouth. Worse, the knowledge that he'd destroyed something beautiful because of his inability to trust and his insecurity about his own feelings, ate at him like a vulture feasting on a carcass.

And that's what he was. A dead carcass with no understanding, no feeling, and no worth.

Perrin shut his eyes, Toni's lovely face haunting his mind. It'd been filled with hurt. Unbelief. Sadness.

Why had he acted like a deranged beast? Just because Marge had been untrustworthy, didn't mean he had to destroy the life in Toni. He groaned and let his head fall forward in defeat.

Chapter Fourteen

Toni shoved open the office door the next morning, feeling its weight.

Roxie looked up. "What's wrong with you?"

"Nothing. Nothing at all. I'm fine. In fact, I'm wonderful." Toni coughed out a brittle laugh. "I'm on top of the world."

Roxie's mouth drew down in a crooked frown. "Yeah, right. I wasn't born yesterday." She lowered her head and gave Toni a stern look. "You look like meat soaked too long in water."

"What an encouragement you are to me."

"Don't twist my words. You know what I mean."

Toni moved toward her office door.

"Secrets have a way of coming out whether we want them to or not."

The words struck her back, and Toni swung around. "What? What secrets are you talking about?"

It was Roxie's turn to look perplexed. "What are *you* talking about? I meant, you don't tell someone who loves you and cares about you, what's bothering you, then there's other ways to find out."

Toni stared at the woman who'd mothered her for years. She would never have made it through the last two years if Rod and Roxie hadn't been here by her side, supporting, loving, and encouraging her. Her heart softened.

Roxie might be brash and bossy, but no one who knew her could doubt her good intentions. If anyone would understand what happened yesterday, it was Roxie. She might chew her out for not listening, but she'd also offer a shoulder to cry on.

She perched herself on the corner of Roxie's desk. "You were right. I went out to the job yesterday, and now Perrin's up in the air again." She looked away, the knife blade nicking at her heart again.

"Didn't I tell you so?" Roxie heaved a sigh. "Rod told me he thought Douglas was tearing into you. He wanted to stop him, but knew you wouldn't thank him for doing so. You just won't listen. If one time..."

"How was I supposed to know he would come at me like a wounded animal?" Toni allowed her shoulders to droop and shook her head. "I can't figure out what his problem is. Someone's hurt that man, and badly. Or else he's mentally off."

"I think you've got that right. I don't know why he acts the way he does, and don't really care. It sounds to me like he's one man who's allergic to women. You might think twice before messing with him again. You've been lucky he's been as friendly as he has, *and* that we even got the job."

"That's a problem." Toni had the grace to look abashed. "He attracts me. The first man in years that's interested me, and he's crazy. How crazy can *I* be?"

Roxie reached over and patted her hand.

"Don't be so hard on yourself. You're not the first woman to fall for a good looking man."

The phone rang, and Roxie answered it. When she'd hung up, Toni stretched out a leg and mused. "He really tore into me. Told me I was untrustworthy and bossy and not to come around the Douglas men again."

"He what? He told you all that?" Roxie's mouth snapped shut. "I think I need to give Mr. Perrin Douglas another call."

"Another call? When was the first?"

"Never you mind. Little girls shouldn't ask questions."

"I'm not..."

"You're my girl. Mine and Rod's, and don't you forget it. When someone hurts something of mine, I hurt."

Toni slid off the desk. "You're worse than a mother tigress."

"Yep. And just as effective."

The morning breezed by. Toni took two calls, both job prospects, finished up the bookkeeping she'd started earlier, and did the correspondence she'd put off forever. When a lull came, she punched the number of the local post office into her desk phone.

"Hi, Jim. Toni DeLuca here. Is there any way to find out who sends mail without a return address?"

"Are you kidding? Probably a fourth of the mail run through here has no return addresses. Unless directly handed to us, we couldn't know."

That was that.

She took time to call Merri Ann again to check on Dr. Felly. Hearing that he was much improved, she set an appointment to visit with him the following week. Only when Roxie paged her that she had a phone call, did she take a breather.

The caller turned out to be Blake, his voice tentative and small. "Toni?"

"Blake? Are you okay?"

"Yeah, I wasn't hurt. Just bruised a bit, but I'm good."

"You didn't have to stay at the hospital?

"Nah. Went home that night." There was a muffled sound as if a door closed, and then he spoke again. "Are you mad?"

"Of course, I'm not mad. Why would you think that?"

"I'm not a kid. I know Dad yelled at you. He had no call doing that to you."

The hurt that had crushed her yesterday rushed in, almost—but not quite—overwhelming her. "I'm fine. You don't have to worry about me."

"Dad's a good dad. He doesn't mean half the stuff he says." Blake's voice held tears in them.

"Of course, he doesn't. I think he's a very good dad to you."

"You do?"

"Yes."

"Dad blames himself because of Mom's death."

"Should you be telling me this?"

"They fought all the time. Big, vicious fights. Mom was always so restless. She never seemed happy. The only time I saw her laugh was when we had company, and she had a bunch of men around her. They loved her." The words tumbled from the boy's mouth, as if he hadn't heard Toni's protest.

"She fussed at Dad about everything. The car was too old. She needed a housekeeper. She wanted to work. I was too noisy. Dad was too busy to take her out in the evenings."

Toni thought her heart would break for his hurt.

"I remember all of them. Every one of her complaints. Even though I was still a kid."

Blake. Was her heart breaking again today for this dysfunctional family of two?

"How can two people marry and hate each other that much?"

Toni had no idea what to say. She opened her mouth, but he rushed on.

"Then that last day, I woke up and heard them screaming at each other. Mom said she wished she'd met a man who could take care of her the way she deserved. Dad said he wished he'd never seen her.

"I found out later, Mom demanded he put new tires on her car, have everything checked and gone over, new brakes, oil changed, and the works. She claimed something was wrong with the car. That if she had to drive old stuff, he could at least have it in good shape. Dad didn't believe her. Told her he'd just had all that done the previous month, and she could wait till he had the time."

The boy's voice choked. "Was it Dad's fault? I love Dad and don't want it to be his fault that mom died."

Toni wanted to cry. What should she say?

"Something *was* wrong with the brakes, and when Mom tore out of the house and later ran off the road, she never had a chance. The cops said she had to be going at least a hundred. She went over a bank. The car went up in flames. We never saw her again."

"Oh, Blake. I'm so sorry."

He sniffed. "I wanted you to know why Dad's like he is. I want you to like him. He's never forgiven himself. Said if he'd been more understanding and given in to her demands, I might still have a mother."

Toni understood. Tears stung her eyes, and her heart melted at the tragedy that had emerged from the Douglas's past. No wonder Perrin was scared of women. No wonder he fluctuated from friendliness to being an ogre. He didn't trust them. Didn't trust himself. His conflicting maze of emotions kept him from forgiving himself and forgetting the past.

Her own roller coaster ride of emotions leveled out as her heart lifted in prayer for this family who were fast becoming important to her.

~*~

The box wasn't that hard to remove from the back of the closet where it had existed since she'd moved in. In it contained the total contents of her past history.

School papers and awards, a trophy, newspaper clippings. Anything and everything about her life growing up. But nothing substantial. Nothing personal that proved her heritage. That she belonged. Nothing that told her who she was.

The small booklet-type album, the cover covered in a childish drawing of her and her dad from years ago, lay at the bottom. She flipped it open and stared at picture after picture. She and Danny DeLuca were featured in almost all of them, with many of their lifelong friends beside them.

Starli and Caro, Toby, Jim, the postmaster when he'd delivered an especially important document to Danny and even Mayor Vicki joined them for that momentous event. There was one where Danny held a three year old, dark haired child—her—with a beaming Dr. Felly beside them.

Some of the people she didn't recognize. Two pictures contained group photos of their church's children club including her dad, Stan, Rita Mae and Sylvia. Toby and Caro had their arms linked around her.

She frowned. Why were her dad, Stan, Rita Mae and Sylvia in the picture if it was a children's club photo?

Digging into her pocket, she dialed Stan's number, and when he answered, asked, "Stan, I have a picture of our children's group from several years ago. Toby, Caro and I were in it. But so was my dad, you, Rita Mae and Sylvia. You all were a little too old to attend our meetings—"

Stan's hearty laugh blared across the airwaves. "I know what you're asking, and that's an easy one to answer. We four were the children directors. Only for one year, and then others took over."

"I see."

Toni sat on the floor and leaned against the closet door, Charms curled in her lap, and thought about her father. He'd been so involved in her life, he'd even been willing to help handle a bunch of rowdy children so he could be there with and for her.

She picked up the picture and studied it. Her dad, Sylvia and Stan were all laughing, but Rita Mae had her usual pout on and stared off to the side. Toni shook her head. She'd never understand the woman.

Closing the lid of the box, she shoved it to the side and pondered. Where was her dad's copy of her birth certificate? Where had she come from?

Appleton had no records on her. Would Charleston?

~*~

Perrin stared at the haggard face reflected in the mirror.

What now? He couldn't work. He'd alienated his son when Blake had tried to take Toni's part. He'd hurt Toni, the only friend he had so far in this town. Why had it come to this? When had everything become such a mess?

When he'd moved to Appleton and met Toni DeLuca.

He'd kept everything so carefully hidden away from the curious eyes of his fellow professors. Those who'd watched the slow deterioration of his marriage. But most of all, for Blake's sake. He didn't need to know the extent of his father's horrible memories.

He'd never forget, but, pray God—if there was a God—his son would never have to live with them.

Perrin paced, peered out his window at the working men below, then returned to the mirror. What kind of a man was he anyway?

Chapter Fifteen

She was slathering apple butter on her homemade wheat toast when the phone rang again. She tossed her knife down and reached again for the phone.

"Toni, want to come over for breakfast?"

Blake Douglas.

"It's seven-thirty. Don't you have to be at school soon?" Toni laughed.

"Two hour delay because of a water break." He spoke in a whispered rush as if to get the explanation over. "I made French toast and Dad's frying the sausages now. Come on over."

Did Perrin know about this invitation? Better proceed cautiously. "Your dad wanted you to call?"

A pause. "Not exactly. It's a surprise for him."

Uh huh. More like a boomerang for her. "I don't think—"

"Don't say no. I *need* you."

Great. How could she say no to a twelve-year-old's plea for help? "Blake—"

"Dad's depressed, and I'm trying to cheer him up. How can I do that if you won't help?"

And he thought her presence would do the trick? The unreasonable deductions of a child. Toni sighed. She was going to regret this.

"All right. If you insist, but only if I can bring something."

"What?" Suspicion pitched his voice a key higher. Perrin's voice in the background said something. "Dad's calling. We've got coffee, milk and orange juice. I've got to go."

Twenty minutes later, Toni walked up the Douglas sidewalk, her arms laden with goodies. The door swung open, and Perrin stood there. From what she could see, her person was not lightening his mood.

"What are you doing here?" To give him credit, he winced. "Sorry. I didn't mean that the way it sounded." Perrin moved forward. "Let me help."

"That's okay. If I relinquish anything, I'll drop the rest." Toni smiled up at him, although her insides were quivering with trepidation.

Moving into the house, Toni leaned forward and eased her burden onto the table. Blake picked up one of her king sized muffins and took a bite big enough to devour half of it. Toni slapped at his hand, and he jumped away, laughing. She pretended to frown. "You'll spoil your breakfast."

"He's already drunk a full glass of juice, stolen one sausage and nibbled at the French toast."

Blake laughed again and tore out of the kitchen, calling, "I'll be right back."

"I gather my son extended an invitation to breakfast?"

Her cheeks warmed as she nodded. "He wouldn't take no. I can leave if you wish."

His gaze rested on her as if to discern her intention. "No, Toni. Stay. For whatever reason, Blake likes you and wants you here, and more than anything I want him happy."

And you don't?

For one horrible minute, Toni was afraid she'd spoken the words aloud. "What can I do?"

Perrin pointed. "Sit. We're the chefs this morning. Might not be as grand as your friend Starli's restaurant, but it'll do."

Toni sank into a kitchen chair, but couldn't help pulling out the blue plaid placemat she'd brought and centering it in the middle of the table. She set the pot of poinsettias on top of it then leaned back to admire the colors and caught the questioning glance Perrin shot her. "Gorgeous, isn't it?"

Blake ran into the room holding a blue and white platter. He dumped the French toast onto it and moved to the table. Perrin slid the sausages onto another platter then poured coffee for himself and Toni, and a tall glass of milk for his son.

When they sat, Blake started to reach for a sausage, but Perrin stopped him. "I have something I need to say."

Would he order her not to return? Give Blake instructions not to invite people to their house?

"I'm not used to doing this. In fact, it's been years since I've backed down, but it is what it is. My behavior yesterday was out of line, and I want to apologize." His eyes met hers briefly before moving on to his son's upturned face.

"Ah, dad, I know you didn't mean what you said."

But had he? His words were stiff and polite, and he had spoken them aloud. She wanted to believe him. The memory of Blake's awful story of his parents burned a hole in her mind.

"Do you mind if I offer a prayer for a new beginning for all of us?"

"I'm not much on prayers." He reached over and ruffled his son's hair, then nodded at Toni. "But if you want, go ahead."

"Are you sure?" When he nodded again, she bowed her head. "Lord, thank you for my friends and their caring enough to invite me to be with them. Give us the strength to develop a strong and lasting friendship. And thank you for this breakfast time together. Amen."

Toni looked up to find Perrin's troubled eyes on her. Ignoring her unease, she smiled. "Are you going to eat all that toast, or may I have a slice?"

The next hour and half passed quickly. When Blake rose to leave, Toni jumped up. "Let me help clean up here, then I'll run you to school."

Blake shook his head. "No, thanks. Sid's mom's taking us. You stay and keep Dad in line." He gave them a cheeky grin, grabbed his book bag and slammed out the door.

A nervous giggle erupted from Toni. She flashed a look at the man sitting opposite. His fingers beat a rat-a-tat-tat, his gaze fixed on the tabletop.

"You mentioned before about my house being unfinished." He hesitated, then plunged on. "What about giving me some ideas on how to finish it up? Since we're doing this addition, we might as well do whatever it takes to make the house look as it should. Get it done now, and I won't have to worry about having it done later. What do you think?"

Toni beamed. "I think that's a fantastic idea. Rod said you'd mentioned it before, and I'd love to help you get it up to par. Are you interested in updating the inside, too?"

"Might as well."

She sat back as the warm feeling stole through her.

~*~

Perrin sat back. He was surprised at the warmth flooding through his body. Toni had that effect on him, but he knew there was something more. Every time he was around Toni, the tight grip he'd held for so long on his bitterness and fear loosened a little bit. Reminding himself to be careful was useless if his heart wouldn't cooperate.

He leaned forward. "Want to look over the house?"

Toni glanced at her watch, debated. "Okay. Let me give Roxie a call."

"The watchdog?"

Toni's mouth twitched in amusement. "Watchdog?"

"Sorry. I got the impression no one would get to you unless they went through her first." He shook his head.

"Oh, yeah. She's a regular mother hen."

After her quick call, Perrin stood and motioned around the room with a sweep of his hand. "What about in here?"

Toni crossed her arms and looked thoughtful. "I'd get rid of the table, put in an island with a range top. You need new cabinets, and I'd go with hickory wood. Over here we could put in a large oven..." she grinned at him, "...for when you have company."

"You're talking a major undertaking."

"Not really. What I've mentioned so far is cosmetic. Your walls are solid. No major structure changes. I think a jade green countertop, and, oh, maybe some touches of spicy-warm orange and brown would be perfect." She nodded her head.

"Sounds good. Can you come up with some swatches so I can see what this is going to look like?"

"I'll do better. I'll draw up a color scheme for your approval."

"Fine." He strode into the hallway. He could hear her footsteps tapping behind him. "Here's the living room."

Toni stood at the doorway and looked back toward the kitchen, a frown on her face. She looked at him. "I take it back. If you really want to open up this place and can afford it, I'd take out this wall..." she indicated the hallway wall, "...and make all of this one room."

"The kitchen in with this?" He knew his skepticism showed.

Toni nodded. "Exactly. We'll put in a partial divider to keep the kitchen separated, but there'll be open space so that those working in there will be connected with your company."

"I'm not too much on entertaining, but I like your thoughts on that. Almost tempts me to entertain."

"Wait till you see the drawing. You'll love it."

"So what about in here?"

"More windows." Toni strode about the room, pointing out her suggestions. "Here, and here. Let's change this slider for French doors. And, what do you think about opening up some of these old fashion fireplaces? A little repair, some cleaning and touchups to modernize them, and you'll have several warm cozy spots throughout your house."

She looked at him, and Perrin could see the hope dancing in her brown eyes. His resistance to her melted like snow on a tropical island. "Great. I've always wanted one. Don't know if I can start a fire."

Toni waved away his doubts. "I'll teach you how with real wood. Or you can have a gas one. This carpet needs to come out, but definitely. Put down a wood floor with some good casual rugs and wallpaper on the walls to give the place some southern class."

Perrin looked at her over his glasses. "We need class?"

"This house does, and it says a lot about you that you chose it. Something about it must have appealed to you."

"Well, I guess my first thought was a quiet place to work. Maybe subconsciously, there were other reasons."

Perrin could see the satisfied smile on Toni's lips as she looked around.

"What else is downstairs?"

"A bath and the room Blake and I share as a study/bedroom."

"No question that needs rectified."

"Agreed."

"Do you have a pantry?" Toni lifted one well-shaped brow.

"I haven't found one."

"Okay. The upstairs is unfinished?"

"Right."

Toni looked positively radiant. "We can probably get at least two nice bedrooms out of that, maybe more, with your own bathrooms. That will leave the addition for your study, and the room you and Blake are sharing for a nice pantry and a small spare room."

"I like it."

The muffled sound of power tools came from outside. Toni cocked her head. "Sounds like the guys are here ready to begin working. I'd better run. I'll draw up some tentative plans for your approval, then we'll study the whole house in more detail after that."

Perrin watched from the front door as Toni left. She stopped to speak to her crew, then swung into her violet truck, giving the horn a toot as she sped down the street.

He shut the door and went to pour himself another cup of coffee, his emotions fluctuating from a sense of rightness, a step in the right direction to a wariness that he was on a precipice. The bell in his brain clanging out a warning didn't help anything.

Chapter Sixteen

Toni walked into Apple Blossoms right on time Tuesday evening. Though their table was empty, she knew Starli would be around somewhere. And Caro would be late—as always.

Manny, the headwaiter, approached her. "Miss Toni. It's good to see you again. How's your friend?"

She looked at him with raised brows. "Friend?"

He touched his lips with a forefinger and hem-hawed. "Excuse me. I thought the gentleman who accompanied you the last time was a friend."

"You mean Perrin Douglas." Toni laughed. "He's a client, but I hope a friend also. He's fine, Manny. Where's Starli?"

A pained exasperation crossed Manny's tanned face. He sniffed. "One of the young ladies came in crying, and, of course, Miss Starli ran to the rescue. As if she doesn't have enough to do."

"You know Starli. Cold demeanor, warm heart." Toni patted his arm.

Manny pulled back a chair at the table he led her to. "I'll let Miss Starli know you're here."

Two minutes later, Starli paused at the edge of the dining room. Her gaze searched the tables, and when she caught sight of Toni, her mouth widened into a smile.

Toni stood to hug her friend, then settled back in her seat.

"Did you get the problem settled with the girl?"

"Camille Findlay. They just found out her mother has cancer. She came into work in spite of that. I sent her home."

"With pay." It wasn't a question. Toni knew her friend.

Starli didn't confirm Toni's comment, nor deny it, but her eyes told Toni the truth.

Fifteen minutes later Caroline Gibson burst in and brushed past Manny who was trying to lead her to their table.

"I'm fine, Manny. Stop your fussing." She called over her shoulder at the man and ignored the glances of the other customers as she swept up to the table and pulled out a chair.

"Hey, you two. Didn't start without me, did you?"

Starli's face brightened. "You know better than that, Caro."

"What's happened?" Toni knew her friend too well.

Caro wrinkled her nose. "Andy stopped by and tried to get me to buy some of his depressing work."

"I take it you didn't?" Starli's teasing tone spiraled around the table, and Toni smiled at their easy banter.

"Are you kidding?" Caro's hazel eyes widened. "I told him no about a hundred times before he got the message. Of course, Toby's not home, so I had to make the decision."

"Andy's a wonderful artist. I can't believe you don't like his work." Toni eyed her.

Caro squirmed in her chair. "Where's Manny? I'm thirsty."

"He'll be here." Starli looked at Toni. "What's going on with you? I haven't talked to you since you were here with—"

"Perrin. He's turned out to be a good client. A very good client." She could hear the smugness in her voice and felt contrite for spreading her news that way. Starli and Caro both stared at her, questions in their eyes.

"Give." Caro demanded.

"He just asked me to redo his whole house." She looked at them to see if they understood the impact of what she'd said.

"December work for your employees." Starli's eyes narrowed.

Caro's eyes widened. "Wow. Is he rich? Better grab him before Rita Mae gets her hands on him."

"Shhh." Starli cautioned and glanced around.

"Phooey." Caro snorted.

Toni grinned. "You already know Perrin's a professor, but he's taken a hiatus to work on his book."

"He's a writer, too?" Caro's mouth hung open.

"For goodness sake, Caro, shut your mouth." Starli snapped, her green eyes brilliant. "Lots of people write."

"Yeah, but a book." Caro argued.

"I think it's impressive." The words were out before Toni could stop them, and two heads swiveled in her direction.

Caro squealed. "Toni. *That* sounds interesting. Just how close are you to Mr. Professor Douglas?"

The red crept up Toni's neck. She knew it. Why hadn't she kept her mouth shut? "He told me about it when we had dinner here. He half promised I could read it."

Starli frowned, then lifted a hand as if to smooth away the frown wrinkles. "I don't trust him."

Toni touched Starli's hand. "He's okay, Starli, you don't have to worry about me."

"I don't want you hurt, and he's hiding something."

The information Blake had shared with her wasn't for everyone's ears. As much as she wanted to help them understand Perrin, she couldn't share it right now. "I can't tell you what his problem is, but he's had his share of trouble and is trying to deal with it. I hope he makes it."

"You like him a lot."

Toni heaved a sigh, then admitted. "Yes. I think I do."

"Does Rita Mae know he's in town?" Caro's eyes sparkled with interest.

I hope not. The words echoed in her mind.

Manny set down their spiced cider.

"You really, really like him." Starli lifted her glass and sipped.

"Yes. Yes, I do. He's boorish and consumed with his work. He's also got the most gorgeous eyes of any man I've ever seen."

Her friends' gazes were intense and filled with curiosity.

"He's big and grouchy and fun to be with when he forgets his past." Toni couldn't help herself, as if the words were pushing to be released.

Starli leaned forward. "I think something else is bothering you. I can't quite..." she paused.

She shouldn't be surprised at her friend's perception. Starli's ordeal with her late husband, Raymond, had given her a heightened sensitivity.

"Is it something to do with that paper Manny gave you?"

"What paper?" Caro's gaze switched between Toni and Starli.

"There was a paper left on one of the tables when Perrin and I dined here. Addressed to me." Toni explained and fumbled in her bag for it. She slid the notes across the table.

Caro leaned forward to scan the paper then lifted one to sniff. "This is a bunch of nonsense. Why haven't you told me?"

"I wasn't going to say anything when I first received the pink card in the mail because I didn't want to believe it."

"I should think so."

"This is absolutely untrue." For such an elegant creature, Starli's snort was definitely unladylike. "No return address? What about the postmark?"

"None."

"Someone local sent it."

"But who? Who would do such a thing to you?" Caro was outraged. "I could see someone doing that to me, but not to you. You are the sweetest person in the world."

"Thanks, Caro. But someone either knows something I don't, or they're playing a very mean trick. Either way, I'm sick over the whole thing. Perrin's offered to look into it."

"He knows?" Starli asked. "You told *him*?"

"He saw the notes when he and Blake stopped by. He's an enthusiastic researcher and figured he could find something."

"That's good of him, considering he's consumed with his work."

"Do you guys know anything? Have you ever heard anything about me, and that maybe Dad's not my biological father?"

Both girls shook their heads. "You look too much like your dad. There's no way you could be adopted." Caro assured her.

"Maybe I'm a relative adopted by Dad and my mother."

"That could be the case, but why doesn't anyone know about it? Did you check with Dr. Phelly?" Starli seldom frowned, but when she did, Toni knew her concentration was at a high level. She was taking Toni's problems seriously.

"I tried, but he's been sick."

"I've got a hunch. I think I may know who's sending those cards." Caro was nodding her head, her dark blond hair bobbing with each movement.

"Are you serious?"

"I am. Let me do a little more searching, and I'll let you know."

"Caro, you have to be careful. He's already threatened my friends."

"You don't have to worry. I'll be careful."

Starli stared straight into Toni's eyes.

"You're Danny's daughter, I don't care what that note said."

"I hope so." Toni sighed.

~*~

"You're going to let Toni renovate the whole house?"

For once he'd shocked Blake. Trust his son to bring out the part of all Perrin's news that was the most important to him.

"It needs done. You need a room of your own, and so do I. Since DeLuca Construction is doing the addition, it makes sense to let them do the rest."

"I told you Toni was good."

Why didn't Blake's smugness rankle like his wife's had? "I thought you and I could go out to eat tonight. Celebrate."

Blake looked at him as if he'd lost his mind. "Celebrate what?"

Perrin strode through the kitchen. "If you insist on a reason, how about: I finished another chapter today. Is that enough?"

When Blake shook his head, Perrin went on. "A new prospective room with a promise from Toni to do the work. Will that work?"

Blake's eyes shone. "Can't we just order pizza?"

"Not tonight. We need to do something fancy. Just you and me. How about Apple Blossoms?"

Blake looked suspicious. "Do I have to dress up?"

"A nice pair of jeans, no holes, and a good shirt and sweater would be good."

Blake grimaced and headed for his room. "I'd rather get pizza. I'm not wearing a tie."

Perrin stared out his window. He hadn't told Blake his real reason. Ever since his brainstorm about the house, he'd felt a load lift from his heart. Not so much from the action itself, but from the effort he'd put forward to do something positive. Maybe it was a start to forgetting his sordid past.

.

Chapter Seventeen

The iced tea slid down his throat, dark and sweet and cold. Perrin pulled the menu closer and studied it. Hmmm. The fresh catfish sounded delicious. He looked up at Blake and started to ask what he wanted. The boy stared to the left at something, a wide smile covering his face. Perrin turned his head to see what had captured his attention.

Toni sat laughing with friends. She, for all her declarations of loving simplicity, looked like a splashy island flower compared to Starli's cool beauty and Caro's homespun looks.

"Did you know Toni would be here, Dad?"

"No, I didn't."

"Can we go over and say hi?" Blake shoved his chair back.

Should they? Would Toni consider them intrusive?

The decision was out of his hands as Blake rushed forward. Perrin followed at a more sedate pace. By the time Perrin stopped at their table, his gaze fixed on Toni, Blake was jabbering to the women as if he'd known them all his life.

Toni looked up, her heart-shaped face alive with warmth and happiness. "Hi, Perrin. I didn't know you'd be here tonight."

He saw her confusion, but she went on. "Not

that I should have."

"It was a last minute decision."

"Dad wanted to celebrate..." Blake began, but Perrin interrupted.

"...celebrate our plans for extensive remodeling."

"We'd ask you to join us, but this is our weekly girl's night out." Caro tilted her head to look up at him.

"That's fine. We just wanted to say a quick hello." Perrin clasped Blake on the shoulder. "Come on, Son, let's leave the ladies to finish their meal."

For the next hour, Perrin fought to keep his attention on Blake. But more than once his gaze traversed the right side of the dining facility to search out Toni DeLuca. Her face was relaxed, her white teeth flashing in wide smiles. She didn't look at him often, but somehow those few glances gave him a sense of ease.

When Blake figuratively licked the last crumbs of his southern fried chicken from his plate, Perrin said, "Want to go for ice cream?"

Blake's gaze flicked to where Toni and her friends stood, saying their good-byes to each other, laughing, and hugging.

"Can we ask Toni to go, too?"

How could he refuse the hopeful pleading in his son's voice? "Why not?"

They met her as she approached the front door. "How about ice cream at The Specialty House?"

Toni's eyes grew huge. "I don't know if I can hold another bite."

"Then come and watch us eat it." Blake

begged.

Her gaze lifted to Perrin.

"Please come." He hastened to add his plea and felt his stomach clench at the familiar warmth her eyes conveyed.

Minutes later, Toni pulled into The Specialty House parking lot as Perrin and Blake exited Perrin's old Chevy, and sat, studying them.

Tall, big-boned men, Blake's hair was sandier and lighter than his dad's, but both had that breathtaking wave in it. They turned in unison toward her truck. Laughing, Blake broke into a run and reached her door first, flinging it open before Perrin had a chance. They vied to walk beside her, giving Toni that exuberant feeling that only came from true happiness. When had she last felt such a thing?

When they'd placed their orders and sat down at one of the fifties retro tables, Toni looked up to see both of them staring at her.

"What?" She lifted a hand to check her hair.

"You're a beautiful woman, Toni DeLuca."

"Thanks. I can't take the credit though." Her saucy reply was said through lips that refused to be disciplined into a serious line. "I think I got an ample share of my father's genes."

"Whoever's to blame for your looks needs to be awarded an award." Perrin's voice was as serious as Toni's had been teasing. "You not only are beautiful of face, but of heart too."

Toni looked down, abashed at the sincerity in Perrin's tone and the warmth in his voice. More than anything, she wanted to believe him, believe that for once he was being honest. "It's easy to love when you've been loved. When you've had such a wonderful life."

"Ah, cut the mushy stuff. I think you're just great. Period."

Who could argue with a preteen's decided and to-the-point statement?

Perrin and Toni looked at each other and grinned. "You're right, Blake."

"Have you learned anything about...?" Toni glanced at Blake.

Blake jumped up. "I'm going to go pick out a song."

"Nothing too wild, please." Perrin called after his son as the boy headed toward the jute box.

"He'll be fine. The owner here allows the kids to hang out and watches out for them by carefully choosing the music they listen too."

Perrin nodded.

"Never had kids, but Rita Mae's great with them." That gave her pause. Why had Rita Mae given up working with the kids? Did it matter? "Have you found out anything?"

"Give me a few more days. I've got a fellow I know digging around some of the local adoption centers. He'll come up with something, I'm sure. Or nothing, which would be even better."

"Okay. I suppose after all these years of not suspecting anything, I can wait a few more days."

Perrin's eyes softened. "It's hard, isn't it?"

Careful.

"I wouldn't let it bother you too much. From what you've said, Danny DeLuca loved you. He's your dad, regardless of what we find out. Family is more than blood, you know."

"I know all that. I just don't want it to be

like that. I want to be the blood part of the DeLuca Family, too. I want whatever heritage Dad passed down to really be mine."

"We'll know something soon. Try not to worry about it."

Toni drew in a deep breath. "I'll try. I've prayed about it and tried to leave it in God's hands. I can't change it."

"Here's our ice cream."

Rita Mae slid Toni's across the table, but leaned over Perrin to set down his dessert. She stared straight into his eyes.

"Hi, Perrin. If there's *anything* at all you want, just let me know. I'm at your service." She winked at Perrin, scorched Toni with a malevolent glare and waltzed behind the counter.

Toni lifted a spoonful of her ice cream and tried not to laugh at Perrin's dumbfounded expression.

"I know I'm not very socially smart, but was that a come on, or am I losing it?"

Toni did laugh then, and Perrin laughed with her.

He stared down at his huge serving of chocolate fudge sundae, then glanced at her skimpy one. "Double chocolate brownie fudge? I thought you couldn't hold another bite?"

"It's been an hour. I think I can handle this."

Perrin lifted his hand and waved, catching his son's eye. He pointed at Blake's own bowl filled to the brim with Appleton's Striped Marshmallow Fluff.

Blake trotted toward them.

Chapter Eighteen

Toni shut her door and made sure the lock was fastened. Charms sashayed down the hallway as if to say, "'bout time you're getting home!" She bent to rub the cat's soft fur. "You been lonesome, Charms? I had the best time tonight."

Straightening, she headed for the kitchen. Her jacket caught on the hall tree where she tossed it, and her shoes landed just inside her bedroom door. She opened her fridge, took out a bottle of water, twisted off the cap, and drank.

Charms curled around her legs. "Hungry, old dear? Let's see. Would you like a treat?" Toni reached for the tin of chicken treats she kept and tossed two of them to the calico.

The cat looked up, blinked her yellow eyes and settled down to devouring the treats. Within seconds, Charms stretched her legs into absurd positions as her pink tongue licked in and out to clean her fur and paid no more attention to her servant.

Toni was exhausted, and Charms trailed along behind her as she headed to her bedroom. As she finished her preparation for bed, Toni yawned, looked down and grinned as the cat opened her pink mouth wide with a yawn of her own.

"We'll worry about our problems tomorrow." Toni sat on the edge of her bed and bowed her head. *God, take these problems and work them out to your glory. Help me be content with whatever happens.*

Toni pulled the covers up to her shoulders, liking the feel of the heavy comforter in the chilly night air. Charms curled at her feet. Drowsiness swept over her, and she smiled, remembering Perrin's words.

You're a beautiful woman, Toni DeLuca.

If only he'd meant them.

Turning to her side, she tucked a hand under her head. Had he meant it?

She almost ignored the creak. But the shadow on the wall caught her sleepy attention, and she raised her head. The next instant a throbbing pain radiated in waves through her head as she fell back against her pillow.

"Don't mess with me. I meant what I said, Toni." The voice hissed in her ear.

Toni squinted at the figure. "Who-o are y-o-u?"

The high-pitched laugh grated on her nerves. Yet through the pain, a faint feeling of recognition knocked against her senses for revelation.

"Don't worry about that. You've got bigger concerns." Another shrill chuckle. "In the morning, when you feel better—and I hope it's not too quickly—check out the paper I've left you."

The pain was overwhelming, and Toni had to fight to keep from passing out. A hand gripped her shoulder and gave it a shake. A nauseating smell assaulted her nose.

Toni lifted a hand and dug her fingers into that hand, feeling her nails slicing into the person's skin.

The hand jerked away, and a half-shriek was a tiny bit of satisfaction.

Returning to her shoulder, the hand tightly squeezed it. An angry voice demanded, "Do you understand?"

She couldn't move her head, but she gave a noncommittal groan.

"Good."

The person gave a quick light tap to the side of her head.

Not enough to injure her further, but enough to send the pain shooting through her head like a quick slice with a knife. Toni slipped into unconsciousness.

~*~

Perrin drove slowly listening to Blake's voice as he chattered about the evening, his interests, and the upcoming remodeling of their home. But his mind remained on Toni.

What an irresistible woman. He'd felt the same way about Marge, and look how their relationship had turned out.

Still, he knew now that Toni was a far cry from his wife.

He pulled into their driveway and watched his son trot to the house and disappear inside. Ignoring the front entry, Perrin walked around the house, climbed the steps, and paused on the large back deck. The two moonlit fruit trees in his yard shone silver in the cold air. Toni's words ran through his mind.

It's easy to love when you've been loved all

your life. When you've had a wonderful life.

How could anyone want to hurt her? She hadn't said much, but he could tell that the possibility of being adopted had hurt her deeply. Tomorrow he would check yet again with Turley. Surely he'd know something by now.

He remembered her declaration of simplicity, and he grinned at the incongruity of her statement. He knew no other woman who confessed that apple blossoms were her favorite flowers. Other women craved driving Mercedes and Cadillacs, while the first woman he'd looked at since Marge's death, loved trucks and antique cars.

She thought the mountain farm haystacks were beautiful, that a fun time was an evening with her girlfriends at Apple Blossoms, and that teaching Sunday school was a valuable part of her life. And though Toni loved all types of music, banjos and fiddles were a normal part of it too. She could get into the hand clapping and foot stomping as easily as the next mountain person.

She had so much love to give. Would the future hold some for—? He couldn't—wouldn't—complete that thought. For now.

Was she in danger? The note-threats indicated it, and someone had run her off the road. His fingers tightened on the porch rail.

The stars shone big and bright in the nippy air and reminded him of the golden flecks in Toni's brown eyes.

With one last look at the midnight sky, he turned to go inside for an hour or two of writing...and to make sure his sleeping son was tucked in for the night.

~*~

Rod pulled into the parking lot right before Toni did three days later. His bushy eyebrows drew together in a frown as he watched her climbing from her truck.

"Howdy, Miz Toni. You sure you ought to be up yet?"

Before she could stop herself, she raised a hand to touch the still-sore spot on the side of her head. "I'm fine, Rod."

"Well, keep that in mind when Roxie sees you here."

"I will." She was so not looking forward to that.

"I've got a bit of news for you."

"Good?"

"Interesting, at least."

She loved this man and his wife. "Well, come on. What are you waiting on?"

Hurrying from the hallway, a pot of water clasped in her hands, Roxie accepted the kiss Rod pecked on her cheek, but her gaze fixed on Toni. "Why are you here?"

Here it came. Roxie sounded as if she was a bit more than peeved.

Toni perched on the edge of Roxie's desk as her secretary settled in her red swivel chair. "I can't stay in bed forever, Roxie."

The red-head sniffed. "It's a wonder you're not dead. Someone trespassing in your home, cracking you on the head, nearly killing you. And if that isn't bad enough, you lying there all alone till morning." She shivered. "What would your father think?"

"I can't hide in the house either. I'm really

all right."

"You're still awfully pale."

"You would be too if..."

"If what, Toni?" Roxie's suspicious eyes demanded an answer. "I knew there was something else wrong with you."

The sigh was deliberate. Now she'd done it. Roxie wouldn't rest until she heard everything she thought Toni might be hiding.

"It's nothing really." Toni frowned as she pulled from a dim memory of things that reminded her of something—no, someone. "Vague feelings I knew the person in my room that night. It's so real I can almost spit the name out, then it eludes me.

Shock registered on both her employees' faces.

"You mean you recognized the person? Why on earth haven't you told the police? It could be the same one who's sabotaging our work."

It was the sharpest Toni had ever heard her supervisor speak.

"That's just it. I can't bring the name to mind, Rod." Toni shut her eyes and thought back to Tuesday night. The smell of perfume rolled over her. Sickening. Distasteful. Familiar. And something she couldn't place.

Roxie pulled out a mirror and patted at her flaming mop of hair. "Well, I don't like it. You're going to have to be more careful."

"I will, Roxie. I promise." Toni glanced at her supervisor. "What's the news, Rod?"

"After I talked with you yesterday, Bob and I kept watch for most of the night at the Douglas job." Rod leaned against Roxie's filing cabinet. "We caught our saboteur last night."

"We did? Rod, that's wonderful. Who was it?"

He held up a hand. "Unfortunately, we know him."

"Kevin."

"'Fraid so. Eddie came running and had him in custody in no time. When I called our good detective this morning, Kevin still wasn't talking."

"Maybe I could question him." Roxie splayed polished nails on the desktop. "I'm dying to do that."

He tweaked her nose. "I'm sure you are, but it's not going to happen, so you might as well stop this nonsense."

"Did you prevent them from damaging anymore of Perrin's material?"

"Broke a couple of boards and disarrayed a few items. But he didn't have time for more mischief."

Toni sighed. If the guy wasn't talking, perhaps he wasn't the main perpetrator. If *he* hadn't planned the sabotage and the theft, then someone was behind it, paying or blackmailing him to do it. It was the only sensible reason. "I don't understand why anyone would do this."

But the image of the threatening notes leaped in her mind. The paper from three nights ago was especially terrifying. She'd stolen an inheritance? It didn't make sense.

As frightening as the paper was, there wasn't a bit of concrete evidence that she'd committed what it declared she'd done. She had no idea how she could have done it, let alone knowing when. It was too vague to be real, yet the threatening tone, after all the other things, chilled her to the bone.

"Exactly."

Roxie was talking, answering Toni's last comment.

"Have you made any enemies, Toni?"

"Before all of this, I would have insisted I hadn't. But now? I can't think of anyone I've ticked off."

"Someone doesn't like you." Roxie eyed her husband. "I bet you think so too, don't you?

"I can't see anyone not liking Toni, but I know something's wrong." Rod ran a hand over his hair. "If I learn anything besides a gut feeling to go on, you two will be the first to know."

Toni nodded. She trusted him to do just that.

"We're both praying, too," Roxie assured her.

"Thanks, you two."

"The guys and I talked about it. We plan to keep watch for the next few days at our construction sites. Just in case Kevin isn't our perpetrator."

Toni rubbed a hand across her forehead. I hate to see the guys doing this for nothing. They've got families to support."

"They're good with it, Toni. Don't you worry about this. You concentrate on figuring out who's trying to...hurt you."

He didn't say it, but Toni knew he was thinking the word: kill.

Roxie nodded. "Someone's called twice asking for you but wouldn't leave a name. We've gotten two inquiries for very nice sounding construction jobs. The inspector for the plumbing at the Nelson job wants to reschedule. And Perrin Douglas called. Asked you call him when you have a minute."

"Will do. Thanks."

At the door to her office, Toni spoke. "Rod, I could take my turn at watching."

"Yeah, right. That's going to happen."

"But I..."

He waved her away. "No. Your daddy would rise up out of his grave if I let you do that."

"Who's the boss here?"

"You are, but even bosses need reined in at times."

Toni retreated to her office and began work on the mail.

If only they'd catch the person soon. She didn't want to live in constant fear of what could be next. Prank or not, she wanted it resolved quickly.

She hadn't talked or seen Perrin in four days. Perhaps he had some good news. She punched in his number, and when he answered, asked, "Aren't you writing today?"

"Maybe. I've tried to call you twice, but your watch dog kept putting me off. What's going on?"

Should she tell? Did she really trust him enough now to spill everything? Why question herself when she already knew the answer? "I've had a bit of trouble."

"Are you all right?"

That was concern in his voice. Couldn't mistake it.

"Someone broke into my home Tuesday night and cracked me on the head while I was sleeping."

"What? Why didn't you tell me?" The outrage in his voice was real and vibrant.

Toni pulled the phone from her ear. Was she hearing him correctly? "Didn't want to bother anyone. But Rod gave me some good news this morning. The guy who's been sabotaging our construction jobs was caught. I'm going down to the jail in a few minutes to see him."

"Not without me, you aren't. I'll be there in fifteen."

The click gave her no chance to decline his presence. But then, she didn't want to.

True to his word, Perrin pulled up in front of the office in fourteen minutes, and they headed to town. As they walked into the station, Detective Eddie met them and led them back to the cell where Kevin sat.

The man barely glanced at her and refused to talk when Toni spoke to him, pleading with him to explain why he'd destroyed so much of her property.

"No use, Miss Toni. Some birds just won't sing. We've got him on destruction of property anyway. Might never know the why."

Perrin clicked his fingers. "I know him."

Deputy Eddie and Toni both stared at him. "You do?"

"Remember the night we had the business dinner? When Rita Mae asked me to meet her friends?"

"Yes."

"He was there."

"There? You mean with Rita Mae?"

"At the table. Rita Mae, her friend, Sylvia, and two other men she never introduced." Perrin grinned. "But she spoke their names.

One of them was Kevin and the other one was the Sal we met." He nodded at her. "Although Kevin looked much neater and stylish than now, it was him. Couldn't mistake those eyes."

She'd seen Rita Mae's table and the other occupants. That is, all but one, which had to have been Kevin. Had he chosen that seat on purpose?

"That is interesting. Why would Rita Mae be hanging around someone like him?"

"Perhaps she didn't know him."

"Hmmm." Perhaps she did. She'd never heard about Rita Mae being in any trouble.

"One thing for sure, Mr. Douglas, that gives us a bit more to go on. We'll be doing some serious interrogating around town now." Deputy Eddie walked them to the door.

Inside Perrin's car, Toni questioned him, "Have you heard from your source?"

She could feel his good mood and smiled in response.

"Maybe. You still planning on attending the Festival Friday?"

"Yes-s-s-s." She drawled out the word.

"Thought I'd ask the prettiest woman in Appleton if she'd take me."

"Take you? Who's going to take her?" Toni teased but pressed a hand to her heart for fear he'd hear it fluttering. Had he really said that?

He matched her tone. "We might be able to bribe someone to do it."

Toni allowed her mock-suspicion to shine through. "With what?"

"How about some good ole Appalachian music?"

"You're on."

When her phone rang, Toni fumbled for it then spoke into the receiver. "This is Toni DeLuca."

At first, there was no sound, then someone spoke. "Toni DeLuca? Is this Toni?"

Toni felt her skin crawl. Who was this? "Yes...?"

"Ah. The little rich girl. *Daddy*'s girl. Look for another card in today's post."

"Why are you doing this?"

A low, throaty chuckle. "It's fun, sweetie. Payback is always fun."

"Why don't you just tell me what you want?"

"Not yet." The voice turned serious. "But soon. Your daddy's a liar, and you're a thief. I'm going to make you pay for it."

"What are you talking about?"

"I'm done playing games."

"I don't—"

When Toni heard the click, she knew the other person had hung up. In slow motion, she hit the end button.

Chapter Nineteen

"I've found three people who use the same kind of pink cards you've been getting."

Caro's triumphant voice bragged into her ear as Toni tied her shoe strings. She sat straight up. "You did?"

"Sure. I've been searching all over town. Sniffing at everyone's stationery, talking to the office supply manager, and finally tracked down three people who use the pink smelly stuff."

"Caro, that's fantastic."

"It was easy. One of them uses them all the time for business. The other two are for more personal things like notes and stuff like that. How dumb can you be?"

Her satisfied grin coming over the air waves was as plain as if she'd stood right beside Toni.

"In fact, I'm holding one right now, sitting here at one of the tables, downtown."

"Caro. Be careful. Now tell me who they are."

With another chuckle, Caro whispered the names.

~*~

On Friday morning, Perrin's manuscript neared completion. Another week, maybe two, and he'd have the first draft finished. After that would come edits and revisions, and he'd be ready to submit to his publisher.

He glanced at the wall clock. Two hours before picking up Toni to head to the winter festival.

Blake had pleaded to have a sleep over at Sid's house from across the street, so Perrin didn't have to worry about getting home for him. He had the whole day to spend with Toni. He leaned back in his chair and stretched.

An hour and half later, he pulled up in front of Toni's house, started to get out when the front door opened, and she appeared. She held up one finger, and he gave her a casual wave and sat back.

In five minutes, she reappeared, meticulously locked her door, then hurried to his car.

He was out and had her door open before she reached it.

"Let's walk."

"You sure?"

"I am. It's not far, and I think it's going to snow. Perfect weather to enjoy. If you're game?"

She grinned at him, teasing, and Perrin felt his spirits soar.

"Blake's spending the night with his friend, Sid, so that frees me up till late.

"I thought they gave the kids the day off to attend. Didn't Blake want to come?"

"Blake insisted he and Sid had plans—something to do with the midwinter science fair and their research for it." Perrin shrugged. He said he'd see me there later."

"Sid's parents are a great couple. Blake couldn't be in better hands." She swung the small basket she carried. "Brought some goodies in case we get hungry."

"I'm hungry now." Perrin eyed the basket. "What's in it?"

"Sor-ry." She held it away from his grasping hand. "You can wait. You had breakfast. I know."

"How do you know that?" Perrin placed both hands on his hips.

"Well," Toni moved closer and reached up to touch the corner of his mouth. "Right there."

He jerked back. "What is it?"

Toni laughed. "Hold still." She used her finger to wipe it off.

He could see her eyes sparkling.

When she stepped back, still smiling, he raised his hand and swiped at his mouth, frowning. "Very funny."

She laughed again. "I thought it was cute."

He gave her a sour look and marched ahead of her. And waited. Then he heard her coming and whirled to face her. "Gotcha, didn't I?"

It was her turn to frown. She narrowed her eyes. "Very, very funny. And mean."

But the merriment in her eyes gave her away.

~*~

Perrin looked at his watch. "I wanted to have a quiet dinner with you this evening, but accepted Sal's dinner invitation. Did you agree to go too?"

"I did."

"Want to go with me?"

"Are you sure?" Toni propped her chin on her fist in mock-pondering. "All day in my company? Sure you can stand it?"

Stand it? Perrin stared at the woman in

front of him. Her teasing brown eyes sparkled at him, the tantalizing mouth widening in a smile he loved. Just weeks ago she'd been the brunt of his antagonism and mistrust. Now?

Now, she was the sweetest person he'd ever known. Nothing seemed to faze her attitude toward her friends and her belief in people in general. "Is that a yes?"

His cell phone rang and after checking it, he spoke in a low voice as he hit the speaker button, "My book agent. I've got to take it. Hey, Jacob, what's going on?"

He could feel Toni's eyes on him, but after the first ten words, he forgot everything but what his agent was saying.

"It's a chance of a lifetime. They want you there first thing Monday morning to talk with the panel of editors, then they've got a tour planned for you to promote your upcoming book."

The agent paused, holding back a tidbit. "Your nonfiction books have incited so much interest, they have big anticipations for your first fiction."

"It's not finished."

"Doesn't matter. Just bring a chapter or two, something to whet their appetite." The guy on the other end guffawed. "I've booked your flight. See you Monday."

Perrin flipped the cell shut and sat staring down at the black phone in his hand. "Looks like I'm scheduled for some heavy promotion for the next few weeks."

Toni's face puckered. "What about Blake?"

Perrin slipped his cell into his pocket and stared at the brick paved street. "I can't take him out of school, not this late in the year."

"Let me watch him. He'll get a kick out of staying in the upstairs of my house." Toni snapped her fingers. "And that'll give Rod a chance to look over things inside your home to get ready to remodel there. I didn't want them to even think about it while you were working on your book."

Perrin nodded. "Are you sure about Blake? He can be rowdy."

"I'm sure."

"I'll talk to Blake and see what he thinks."

"What about your book? How can you get it done with all that on your agenda?"

"I'll have to press for personal time to work on it. I can't let them schedule too tightly."

"That's good. I hate..." she paused, and Perrin looked over at her. Did he hear concern in her voice?

"You hate what?"

"I don't want you to be so busy you can't get done what's on your heart. Is it really necessary to do all that promoting and to be gone for so long? You might like it so well you'll never return permanently."

Was she serious? What a contrast this woman was with his wife. Nothing could keep him away. "I doubt that. I'm really not a social climber. I like my solitude too well. But Jacob thinks it's important for me to do this. And I realize that it's a great opportunity. I can't turn it down."

"I guess so." Toni pleated the edge of her jacket, then pulled the paper bag she'd placed at her feet onto her lap. "Here. I've got something for you."

He took it and unwrapped the tissue paper. The figurine sat snuggly in his palm.

"It reminded me of you." Toni looked at the small figure of a man sitting at a desk, writing, then up at him.

"Thanks."

"Do you like it?"

"Yes, I do like it. Especially that it's locally made. I'll sit it on my desk and think of you when I look at it."

"I didn't give it to you for that reason."

"I know, but it's what I want to do." He reached for her hand and squeezed it.

Chapter Twenty

Toni twisted her hair back in a knot at her neck, eyed herself, then shook out her curls. Nope. Starli could get away with that classical style and look elegant, but not her. She pinned her hair in a topknot, allowing several curly strands to free-fall around her face. Pinned a large gold hair clasp in her hair. Much better.

The attraction she felt for Perrin continued to bloom inside her despite her determination to starve it to death. The nagging concern about his lack of interest in church disturbed her. She'd tried to ignore it, tried to reason it away, but every time she did, Pastor Stan's concerned words Sundays ago, replayed through her mind.

She could never have a perfect marriage if she and her husband didn't pull in the same direction. Both man and woman needed to love God. Together.

And she knew if it came down to it—if their relationship developed into more than friendship—she would have to make a tough decision.

Toni walked slowly into her living room and stood at the front window staring out at the front street. Charms came up beside her and wound her body around Toni's legs. She bent to stroke her cat's soft hair, murmuring to her.

She enjoyed being friends with Perrin and

Blake. They were smart and interesting and challenged her intellect with their ready comments to counter her statements. She loved listening to their mild father-and-son disagreements and their friendly jokes that sometimes only they understood. She adored their identical lopsided smiles and teasing eyes, both of them with their too-big glasses.

The sound of an engine reached her ears. Toni watched as Perrin pulled up, swung out of his old car and strode toward her door. Halfway there, he shifted his gaze to the window and saw her.

Her cheeks warmed as his face lit. There was such real delight on it, such neediness for trust, embarrassment swept over her at the naked emotion. Behind the wire-rimmed glasses, his eyes shone with happiness. One side of his mouth curved up higher than the other, and his teeth glinted white in the semi-darkness of the winter night. He lifted a hand.

What a difference a few days had made in him.

She strode to the door and paused, her head resting on it. *Dear God, don't let me do anything to ever hurt Perrin. He's been hurt enough.*

When she heard his soft knock, she flung it open. "Hi, there."

"Ready?"

"Yes-s-s-s." She hurried to grab her shawl, shooed Charms away from the door, and closed it behind her. "I'm ready."

Perrin held out his arm, and she tucked her hand within it.

"Then let me put my princess into her

carriage."

She gave him a side-ways glance. Had he really called her *his* princess? She swallowed.

As they took off, Toni asked, "Blake still okay?"

"You mean staying with Sid?"

She nodded.

"He's fine. You've quickly become one of his favorite people. Awesome is his one word description."

Happiness spread through her.

"Pretty accurate, I'd say."

Perrin's low words as he pulled into Apple Blossoms tingled her skin. Toni wasn't quite sure she heard him right. Had he said what she thought he said?

Inside, Manny showed them to the private room Sal had booked tonight, led them to a long table, then took their drink orders. Starli was seated at the piano, smaller than the main room instrument, but just as well tuned. Her limber fingers glided over the keys—coaxed out the music she loved from it—the musical romance breathing into the room.

"Wonder what's Sal's real purpose is inviting a select few." Perrin spoke in a low voice meant for Toni's ears only.

"I don't know, but perhaps we're about to find out. Here he comes," Toni whispered back.

The man weaved his way straight to their table. Perrin stood as he approached, and Sal nodded at him, but his gaze focused on Toni. "My dear, you are divine tonight."

What woman wouldn't like that compliment? Toni grinned at him. "Are you talking to me, Mr. Sal?"

He lifted her fingers, and unlike before, kissed them. "I am."

The smoldering flame in his eyes held her captive for a moment longer than she liked, but she broke free and lifted her glass to sip from it. "Thank you, kind sir."

"Then after I greet my other guests, I'll be back to talk with you." He nodded and turned away.

Sylvia and Rita Mae claimed him, both chattering as if they'd seen him before.

"I'm afraid I don't care too much for that man." Perrin's voice was as low as it'd been before.

"Oh? Why not?" She was playing with danger, teasing Perrin, but she wanted his reaction. Was he jealous that Sal had singled her out? She decidedly hoped so.

Perrin scowled. "So overdone, that accent and those elaborate manners. I can't seem to accept him as real. There's something about him—"

He stopped, and Toni looked at him. "I agree."

"You do? I thought..."

"What did you think?" Toni laughed at his woe-be-gone expression. "Do you think I'm so fickle that every man who tries to woo me sways me?"

"I don't think you're fickle at all. I told you, I think you're—"

"I know what you said. I'm teasing you again." Toni allowed her eyes to express what she meant. "But I am interested to find out why I'm the only woman in the room that he felt a need to kiss her fingers."

"So you noticed?"

"Of course. And if you'll forgive me for neglecting you, I'm going to do my best to find out why tonight."

Perrin touched his forehead with two fingers. "Aye. Aye, Captain. More power to you. I think I'll take a stroll over to the piano and make friends with your friend Starli. I see Sal headed this way."

"Shall we stroll about a bit? I've given instructions to hold our dinner for a half hour or so. Better to socialize a little and give me a chance to know you better." Sal took her hand and placed it on his arm.

"I'd love to. Sitting too long is a bore to me."

The man smirked. "I thought so. I see that our entertainment tonight is quite the accomplished pianist."

"She is. Starli is talented."

"Tell me about my guests."

"You want me to gossip?" In spite of her serious doubts about the man, Toni had to admit he was quite the charmer.

His amused gaze studied her reaction. "Ah, does that bother you?"

"I'm not used to spreading vicious tales."

He laughed. "Then, by all means, do not do so. I wouldn't want to be the one to encourage such—what should I call it?—misdemeanors."

It was Toni's turn to laugh. "I don't mind sharing a few tidbits though."

"Ah, wonderful. I have a purpose in asking, you know."

"I'm sure you do." Toni hoped the dryness wasn't quite as loud in her tone as it seemed to be to her ears. "Starli, of course, you know is the owner of Apple Blossoms. You met Perrin Douglas the other night when Rita Mae invited him to her table for a few minutes."

"I have been wondering ever since why the invitation was not extended to you also."

That would take a little more explanation than she was willing to go into. "Suffice it to say, I'm not her favorite person."

"Hmmm." He tapped his chin. "I see."

What did he see? "Rita Mae, I assume you know, owns The Specialty House. She serves the best coffee in West Virginia, and her ice cream is locally made. She's a very good business woman."

"And her friend, Sylvia Searles?"

"She works for a local insurance agency and has one son, Arnie."

"Do I hear reservations in your tone?

"Nothing against Arnie. He's a wonderful friend to me."

"I think there is one thing my friend is holding back."

Toni sighed. "Sylvia has had a bee in her bonnet. She's obsessed with the desire to push Arnie and me together."

"But you are not compatible?"

"I'm afraid not. I love Arnie dearly as a longtime friend, but our relationship will never go further."

"Yet he glances yearningly in our direction."

Warmth crept up Toni's neck. "I hope not."

Sal led her to a tall window and paused beside it. "Do you know the rumors that are spreading?"

"Rumors?"

"About you."

"Me?"

"That you are sabotaging your own business to claim insurance money."

The Italian temper rose. "What are you talking about? Who said such a thing?"

"Don't blame the messenger." Sal lifted a hand, then reached for hers to replace it on his arm. He grimaced. "Now it is my turn to spread what you call vicious gossip, is it not?"

"Do you or do you not know who started this lie?"

"I do. But first, I want to make you an offer."

"An offer. What kind?" Toni's mind went blank.

"As soon as I saw you, before I was introduced, I knew you were the type of woman I admired." His voice dropped even lower. "I'm expecting, if all things go as I want, to come into quite a bit of money soon. To fulfill my plans, I need the right people beside me."

That made sense, but what did it have to do with her? Was he asking her to help finance a project and wanted to make sure she was solvent?

"Antonietta DeLuca, will you marry me?"

~*~

"I've got news."

"News?"

"About..." he lowered his voice "...the adoption business."

"How could I forget? Tell me quick."

"Turley did a lot of digging. He had a couple of resources that owed him a favor. What he found was nothing."

What kind of news was that? Toni looked at him. "What do you mean?"

"He didn't find anything proving you'd been adopted. Of course, no one would tell him any names, but the questions he asked were all answered. And nothing matched. Nothing at all. In fact, there is only one legitimate adoption agency in the state. Turley checked all the surrounding states, and then used his resources for state records. Absolutely nothing."

Toni could see Perrin was pleased with the results, but she wouldn't give herself that satisfaction yet. There were too many variables here. "What about a private adoption? You know, between a couple and an unmarried girl?"

"There is that. There's no way to know everything. But as far as he could go, Turley went. What percentage could it be that something like that happened?"

"If there is a one percent, I could have been in that one percent."

"To make it legal, it'd have to be recorded in the state records."

He was right. But the niggling doubts prodded.

She laid a hand on top of his fingers. "Thank you. At least we know that much. You've been great. Will you thank Turley for me? Do I owe him?"

Perrin waved away her question. "Don't worry about it. I just wish you wouldn't fret so much about what you can't know."

"Wouldn't you want to know for sure?"

"Maybe."

Manny placed their salads in front of them and waited silently.

"What is it, Manny?"

"Miss Starli wished me to ask what you would like to hear tonight?"

Perrin leaned forward. "What about 'Brown Eyed Girl'?"

The head waiter looked at Toni, and she nodded at him.

"Do you mind?"

"Of course not. I've requested dozens of songs from her."

As Starli played the opening chords, Perrin spoke in a low voice, "It reminds me of you."

~*~

Perrin pulled into her driveway, and Toni was surprised when he shut off the engine. He turned in his seat, propping his arm on the back of it.

"Toni. I'm not a man to trust easily, and I judged you harshly from the first. But I can't ignore the attraction I feel for you. Do you feel the same?" He paused, waiting on a word from her.

Toni felt her heart stop. This was what she'd been waiting for, wasn't it? She owed it to him to be honest. "Yes, I do, Perrin. More than I have for any man."

Her pastor's message from last Sunday played over in her mind. Take it slow. Make sure the person you're interested in, has a commitment to God matching yours.

The words rang in her ears. Here was the test. What would she do? She couldn't answer *his* specific question without more commitment from him. She needed to know he wanted to put God first in his life.

"You have to leave early Monday morning.

Could we spend Sunday together?"

"What do you have in mind? Church? Dinner? An afternoon walk?"

Even in the darkness, Toni could feel the sudden strained atmosphere.

"Something like that. Is that too much for me to ask?"

"Does your request have something to do with our relationship deepening?"

Toni gazed at him, willing him to see the answer in her eyes.

"Have I hindered Blake in going to your church? Have I tried to discourage you?" His words were low. He stared out the window, his gaze fixed on something beyond the car.

"No."

"I'm trying hard to change my attitude, and I've succeeded, I think. You've become a friend that I value." He threw open his door. "But I'm not ready to commit to church. Yet."

Toni watched as he trotted around the front of his car. He opened her door, almost gallantly, and she stepped out. His hand gripped hers.

"I won't be pressured into making a commitment I can't keep. I may never make such a commitment. I wasn't raised in church, Toni, and I've got to decide for myself if I want it to be a part of my life. You've got to give me that."

He didn't give her a chance to answer, only tucked her hand in the crook of his arm and walked her to her door. When she'd inserted her key, and shoved the door open, he raised her hand to his mouth and breathed out his next words.

"I won't see you again before I leave. If you still want Blake, I'll have his things ready. Thanks for the evening." He kissed her hand, then dropped it and turned away.

Toni watched him. She hated that her eyes stung from hot tears. She feared things would never be the same again.

Chapter Twenty-one

A week later, Toni headed to Dr. Felly's home. When she'd last talked with Merri Ann, she'd given her hope that the favorite pediatrician in Appleton would soon be physically able again to talk with her.

She pulled up to the aged farmhouse with its screen doors and peeling-painted pillars. Two German shepherd dogs galloped up to her truck, tails wagging, barks loud and scary, if she hadn't known what babies they were.

Toni tumbled out of the truck, fell to her knees and caressed the short stiff hair of each dog before rising to her feet. She, accompanied by the dogs, strode to the porch. Merri Ann flung open the door as Toni approached.

"Come in. Come in, child. Nippy this morning, isn't it?" Merri Ann's ample arms reached out to pull her close for a hug. "Haven't seen you for a long time. Where you been?"

She led her toward the living area, her chatter lively and filled with inconsequential information about their favorite patients. Things that kept the two older folk involved in the community.

"Dr. Felly, here's Toni DeLuca come to see you." Merri Ann raised her voice.

Toni followed the older woman into a

Carole Brown

flowered wallpapered room. At one end, near a fireplace, sat an older man, a coverlet covering his legs. He turned his head, and a wide smile lit his wrinkled face. "Antonietta. Come." He motioned with one hand.

Toni hurried forward and bent to give her childhood pediatrician an affectionate hug. "How are you, you dear?"

Dr. Felly's brisk, loud voice bellowed, although Toni could detect a shakiness that hadn't been in it the last time she'd seen him. "I'd be fine if that woman, who thinks she's my nurse, would let me back in my office."

Toni laughed and pulled up a nearby stool. "You need to take care of yourself."

He peered at her, his eyes narrowing. "Since when did you become a doctor?" He harrumphed. "Telling your old doctor what to do. Fine howdy-do."

Toni patted his arm. "I've come to talk with you."

"You're not sick, are you?"

"I'm okay physically." Toni twisted her fingers together, suddenly nervous about what she wanted to ask him.

"Well, speak up, child," he ordered her in a gruff voice, but Toni knew that underneath that rough exterior, lurked a tender caring heart.

Toni sat for a moment, then looked at the man beside her. "Dr. Felly, how long were you my childhood doctor?"

He shook his head. "Child, I can't remember the years. But it's been a long time."

Tear stung her eyes. "When I was a baby? Were you my doctor right after I was born?"

Something in her voice must have alerted him to her mental state, because he was at once serious, his voice gentle. "Toni DeLuca, what are you asking me? Tell me now."

"Dr. Felly, I need to know. Was Danny DeLuca my real father, my biological father?"

He didn't answer, and Toni held her breath, both afraid and anxious for what he might say. He closed his eyes and tilted his head back. Toni kept her gaze fixed on his wrinkled face, her heart growing more fearful.

At last he opened his eyes, raised his voice. "Merri Ann. Get me Toni's file."

"What?" Merri Ann's shoes squeaked on the clean wooden floor, then her round body appeared in the doorway. "Did you want something, Dr. Phelps?"

"Get me Toni's file now." He snapped at her, then grumbled to Toni. "Slowest woman in the world. I ought to fire her and get me one of those younger, up-to-date nurses."

Toni smiled knowing Dr. Felly would no more get rid of Merri Ann than he would cut his hands off.

Two minutes later Merri Ann bustled in holding a large sloppy folder, which she placed on the card table she pulled close to the doctor. When she hovered, he motioned her away.

Toni scooted closer.

He opened the file slowly, flipping through several pages. At last, he turned to the back of the file and eased an envelope out from under two large paper clips where it'd been clasped. He held it up, stared at it.

When she looked at her, he spoke. "I've had

this for a great many years. I was instructed to give it to you on one condition."

Toni couldn't speak, her gaze pleading with him to tell her.

"I was to give this to you if and when you ever came to me asking questions. If I died before that time, it was to be destroyed."

"But why? Why destroy something I might need or want to know?" Hurt and puzzlement ran through her like the swollen mountain streams in springtime.

Dr. Felly's head moved back and forth in slow motion as if the instructions were a puzzle to be solved by him, too. "I don't know, child. But I think your father…"

"Daddy gave this to you?" Toni interrupted and heard the echo of her breathless voice.

"Yes, your daddy came to me one day and asked me to keep it for you, if the time ever came when…" He hesitated and coughed. "…when you approached me, like today. I think your father hoped you'd never come."

"Why would he hope such a thing?"

The old man looked at her, and Toni saw the tears. "He loved you so much. You were the light of his eyes. He didn't want you to have even one troubling moment in your life. My guess is, he hoped you'd never have any questions."

Toni stared at her hands, clutched in her lap, emotion overwhelming her voice. At last she whispered. "Thanks, Dr. Felly."

He leaned forward, placed a gnarled hand on hers. "Don't you forget what I told you now."

She gave him a shaky grin. "I won't. I promise."

Her knees wobbled as she walked to her truck, climbed in, and turned the key. She laid the envelope beside her, knowing that whatever it contained could change the way she thought about her life forever. For a wild moment, she considered ripping it into pieces, then common sense returned.

She put the truck in gear and drove home.

Once home, Toni held the envelope in her hands as she walked through her home, then returned to the front room again, Charms trailing behind. She envisioned her father's face. Happy and handsome. But now that she was here with the letter, could she open it? Could she face it if her father told her she was adopted?

She fed Charms, replenished her water bowl, brushed out her fur. Then, after showering, she prepared supper, all the while conscious of the envelope lying on the countertop right beside the pink cards with all the hurtful words. But she was determined to read it in her own time.

When she was ready. When she'd finished her evening chores. Right before bedtime. Or not...

Here she was, at home, torturing herself by waiting to open the envelope.

Or was it she was too afraid?

Her hand hovered over the envelope, and then she jerked it back as if she'd just touched a coal from her fireplace. She moved to her plate of tenderloin and mixed vegetables she'd canned this autumn, and raised a forkful to her mouth.

Ten bites later, she shoved her plate away,

placed a couple of cookies on a small plate, and poured herself a cup of coffee. Then gripping the envelope under her elbow, she juggled the plate and coffee cup to her fireplace.

Setting them both on the hearth, she threw down her favorite supersized pillows, and eased herself down, sitting cross-legged. She took a bite of a cookie, a sip of coffee, then reached for the envelope.

It was time.

Her fingers trembled causing the envelope to shake, but she slapped her hand onto the hearth. "Stop it, Antonietta DeLuca. Just stop it. Whatever's in that envelope will not—cannot change who you are. You're still you. Remember what Perrin told you? And Starli and Caro?"

Toni looked at the phone resting on a nearby end table. She could call one of her friends, but did she want anyone, even them, here right now?

No, she decided, this was a time for privacy.

She lifted the envelope again and inserted her finger under the flap.

The envelope, for all its years of being sealed, unfolded without tearing. Trepidation filled her heart. Carefully, she pulled out the sheets of paper and unfolded them. Something fell to her lap, but her gaze dropped to the signature at the bottom of the sheet.

Forever your dad,
Danny Deluca

Toni gasped, and even though she'd known who had written the letter, a hand of longing squeezed her heart, jerking her back to the past.

She'd never been rebellious growing up. Her father, so understanding, so influential on her that she'd never had serious desires to rebel from the few no-breaking-them rules he'd laid down.

Not that she'd been perfect. No. But compared to Caro—and even Starli—she'd been tame. The few escapades she'd taken part in had fizzled out with Danny's discernment of what was youthful nonsense or a miniscule piece of rebellion on her part. Though at the time, she'd not been keen on such super discernment, now she realized what great wisdom he'd displayed.

He'd been almost too wonderful to be a father. Joining in her fun, or searching her eyes with his own steady, probing gaze when there was any question about the appropriateness of the situation she was involved in. He'd been there, a steady bright light in her life.

She picked up the fallen paper and realized it was a photo. A young woman, barely out of childhood, stared at her, a hint of a smile on her lips, her blue eyes serious—almost too much so. There was no name on it, but Toni felt her fingers convulse as she gripped the edges.

Then she looked at the letter and began reading.

My dearest Toni,
I hope you never read this.
But in the event that you do, please remember that I love you, that you've always

been the light of my eyes.

I've only decided to write this recently because of a remark made to me, and I realized I needed to put this on paper for you, in case. You'll read in here several things we've never spoken of. Not because I didn't want you to know, but because I wanted your life to be happy and filled with perfect memories. I don't want anything negative to bother you. So if some facts in this letter to you are disturbing, I'm so sorry. I never meant to hurt you.

Why am I writing this letter to you? Of course, you're asking questions, or you wouldn't be reading this. And I have a great desire to live a long, long time, to share in your finding the right companion—if God so wills—and seeing my grandbabies. But I know that things don't always turn out the way we want them to. So just in case I die before all that, and you ever have questions, this letter is to put those questions to rest.

And remember, I love you. Always.

Here's the story.

Your birth mother's name was Sandra Jones. Sandra—never Sandy—was a lovely person and, occasionally you move your head or say something that flashes me back to her actions.

Sandra and I met one summer when I passed through Appleton. I wanted to see the world, but instead saw Sandra Jones. She was staying with her grandparents in their summer home, and we fell in love. Or, at least we thought we did.

Sandra's family was very, very strict. Very, very old, with descendants dating back farther than the Revolutionary War. They were snooty, but I reckon they had a right to be. They hardly let her out of their sight, always afraid she would be tempted or led astray by some wicked person.

Well, that summer, I was that wicked person. I take all the blame on myself. She was innocent and sweet, shy, but a little bit wild and hungry to experience life. And we did.

We did, Toni.

In the fall, Sandra went home without letting me know she was leaving. I didn't hear from her again. I wanted to keep in touch, wanted to write and go see her, but her cold grandmother absolutely refused to tell me where she lived. Over the next few months, I met another girl, married her, and we settled in Appleton. Leah Morris. Your stepmother and the woman who gave me six wonderful married years.

It wasn't until my boss, who knew old man Gerald Jones, the grandfather, as a business associate and distant family member, spoke about the Jones' granddaughter having a baby girl that I realized Sandra had become pregnant through our actions that summer. He'd heard the tale making the rounds in the family.

I was frantic. How did I know I was the father? I didn't for sure at first, but calculating on the calendar led me to feel I was no doubt to blame for Sandra's pregnancy.

I began my search for Sandra. One day in Charleston, where I was working, I happened (God?) to see Mr. Jones, the grandfather, downtown. Without thinking I approached him and begged him to tell me where Sandra was.

Now remember, I was just nineteen and Sandra sixteen the summer we met. After I met *her, I began working for a big time contractor. I did pretty good, had my own apartment, and a little put by for a rainy day.*

Back to Mr. Jones. He stared at me with his cold gray eyes, his thin lips pressed together in contempt. But as I babbled on, begging, all of a sudden, I saw something soften in his eyes. He didn't say anything. When he walked away, he dropped something. I stared after him, heartsick.

On the ground lay a card, and I stooped to pick it up. What I read, sent my heart and spirit soaring. It was Sandra's parents' address.

I wasted no time in contacting her. Sandra couldn't do anything but cry. I promised to send her money, to help her get her own apartment.

But something happened. Sandra had never told me she'd had heart trouble from childhood. Her pregnancy had been too much for her. Two months after our reunion, she passed away.

At first, the Jones' family balked about letting me have you or even letting me see you again. I wouldn't stop, and really, Toni, they had no desire to raise another child. Sandra's parents were involved in their own world of business and had no time to raise a baby.

It took me two years, with DNA testing and court appearances, but finally, finally, I prevailed!

Can I describe how I felt when I held my child—you!—in my arms for the first time? You were two and a half, and beautiful. Sandra had remarked you looked like me. Your hair was dark and curly, your eyes big and brown. You were a good baby, but active and alert. We loved you dearly and were so proud of you.

I took you back to my home after gaining custody of you. It was small for the three of us (Leah, you, and me), but we managed. By the next summer, we were able to put a good down payment on a bigger place. A year later, I went into business for myself. The DeLuca Construction Company.

Six months after that your stepmother, Leah, died unexpectedly, and we were alone.

Toni, dear, your birth mother loved you. She cried when she knew she would have to leave us. She held you constantly right up until the time she became too weak to do so. Then we placed your bed in the room where she could watch you. You played at the foot of her bed and on the big oval rug on the floor beside it.

I've tried hard to be both mother and father to my dear girl. I think I didn't do such a bad job. You're intelligent and hard-working, sweet and kind, a good upstanding citizen, a real Christian in the community. And a wonderful daughter.

Why did I write this letter? Because if you ever had any doubts about anything, anything at all, I wanted you to know the answers. Although we were young and sinful, never doubt that we both loved you more than anything. There was never a time we didn't want you, in spite of everything.

My prayer is that you will have a wonderful family with a man you love and can't live without, and if God so wills it, children who are as much of a blessing to you as you've been to me.

Forever your dad,
Danny DeLuca

Toni's fingers clenched the papers. She lifted one hand and touched her wet face.

She wanted to call Starli and Caro, but stopped herself. Tonight was hers. Hers and Danny's...and Sandra's.

Chapter Twenty-two

It'd been over a week since Perrin had talked or seen Toni. In that week he'd flown to New York, met with the panel of editors who'd entertained him with dinners and special meetings to explain their promotional ideas. He'd been so busy that he'd had no time to think of anything but work.

Now he sat in his hotel room, his laptop open, but his thoughts back in Appleton. All of a sudden, such a fierce longing for home and Blake and...Toni swept through him, he felt physically sick. For a crazy moment, he was tempted to throw everything overboard and take the next flight home.

That was out of the question. He hadn't come this far, worked this hard to throw it over. And nothing had changed in his heart. He couldn't, wouldn't make a commitment—a choice—he didn't want to keep. He had to know for sure that he wanted Toni *and God*, more than anything.

~*~

Toni placed a firm tomato on her cutting board and pulled out a sharp knife.

The foundation of Perrin's addition had been laid and the walls were up. Toni was delighted with their progress, and though Perrin had changed his mind twice over the window locations, they'd worked with his desires.

Toni had bent over backward to make sure he got what he wanted. She didn't want him to accuse her of interfering. She felt more at ease with him, but still, there was no need to rock the boat.

And if there was to be any more furthering of a relationship, it would have to come from him. He was no dummy. The next move was his.

She sighed. Her knife slid through the tomato, and she flipped it to make another slice. Tacos for dinner. She hoped Blake liked them. She glanced at the cheese she'd grated, the onions diced and ready, the lettuce torn into bite sized pieces. The sour cream was in the fridge, the meat sauce on the stove bubbled its rich, seasoned scent into the air.

Her heart was light that there had been no more vandalism at the construction site.

But something bothered her. Tossing her knife to the counter, she gave her ingredients another glance, checked her simmering sauce, then headed to her bedroom. The box of her life-long mementos still sat crookedly on the far side of her bed. Plopping to the floor, she pulled it close and lifted off the lid.

The envelope filled with pictures lay on top, and Toni picked them up. Kneeling at her bed, she dumped the whole bunch onto the coverlet and scattered them. Then she picked up one and stared at it.

It was of her and her father standing in front of a solid wooden door. There were no windows, and it looked like it could withstand an army of intruders or the roughest storm. Toni ignored the father and child-daughter, the door demanding all her attention, forcing her to remember...what?

Closing her eyes, with a prayer on her lips, Toni let her mind wander back and back. That door...she almost had it...

Vaguely, from the hidden recluses of her mind, a shadowy memory immerged. Sometime in the past she had visited that house. There had been no laughter, only unpleasant sensations of coldness and displeasure.

Her great grandparents, the Joneses, had lived in that house.

...Their summer home...

The words from her father's letter rushed at her and fell perfectly in place.

And what was even more surprising—she'd seen that house recently. It now belonged to Perrin Douglas. That's why his home had seemed familiar. The present door had thrown her off. It wasn't the one her mind had sealed within her memory.

Shuffling the pictures, she picked up first one and then another. Then she paused and slowly lifted another. It was a family picture— or at least she assumed so. Her great grandparents and two other people whom she figured could be her grandparents, a teenaged girl with a messy head of brown hair, crossed arms and an air about her that said, 'Don't mess with me,' stood between another couple. Danny Deluca held his daughter, and he was the only one of the bunch who looked even remotely happy.

What a horrid bunch of people. Except her dad, of course.

The door banged open, and Toni heard

Blake sauntering into the kitchen. She hurried back to the kitchen and was just in time to see him snitch a shred of cheese.

Slapping at his hand playfully, she ordered, "Go wash your hands, then come and help me set out places."

"Can't we eat in front of the fireplace?"

"Not tonight. These are too messy. But we'll have dessert there. How about that?"

Blake disappeared into the hall. She heard his footsteps clattering up the stairs. The bathroom door banged, and the sound of running water reached her ears.

Ten minutes later he was back. He'd changed his shirt, and he'd obviously tried to curb the curl in his hair with water. Toni directed him with a tilt of her chin. "In that cabinet—no, not that one. The one next to it. That's it."

Blake set the places at the island and placed napkins and silverware. He opened the fridge and reached for a can of soda. Toni stopped him.

"Sorry, dear. Better drink milk tonight. Didn't you have pop with your lunch today?"

"Yeah." Blake's sheepish eyes met Toni's, then flicked away.

"Your dad said no more than one a day. Remember?" Toni scraped the diced tomatoes into a green bowl. "Did you and Sid have a good practice after school?"

Blake nodded and poured his milk. "Toni?"

"What, dear?"

"Why hasn't dad called?"

That was a question she'd like answered too. "I don't know. You know his editors have him booked pretty heavy. I'm sure he's very busy. He'll call as soon as he can." She looked at the boy's averted face. "You miss him?"

"Yeah."

She dished up the sauce and sat on a bar stool beside Blake. After the blessing, he dug in, finishing off two rolled up tacos before she had half hers gone. He looked up as he chewed the last bite.

"These are de-lish! Best I've ever eaten."

"It's the homemade sauce. I put in fresh spices and allow it to simmer for a couple hours." She swallowed her own bite, laid her taco down, and wiped her hands. "Have homework tonight? Any plans with Sid?"

"Nah." He leaned his head against a palm, a sudden bored expression rippling across his face. "Sid's family's going away this weekend. I've only a few pre-algebra problems to finish and a report to do. I can get that done in the morning." Curiosity bloomed in his eyes. "Why?"

"The park is all decorated for Christmas, and the pond is frozen. Let's go there tonight." Toni shook her hair from her shoulders and wondered if she'd regret what she was about to say. "I haven't ice skated forever, but thought I'd like to try my hand at it again if you'd like. Are you game?"

Blake jumped to his feet, almost overturning his stool. "Am I? I'm the best. When can we leave?"

Toni laughed. "Don't you want dessert?"

He tore out of the room, his voice floating back to her as she stood to clear the counter. "Later."

~*~

The park was lit with a multitude of lights giving it a fairyland look. Couples walked arm in arm, others jogged along the paths out for their evening exercise, and twosomes strolled together, singing along with the music piping into their ears. Several kids rolled enormous snow balls into snowmen.

At the frozen pond, some had their ice skates on and whizzed by as she tied up her rented ones. Blake sat beside her and fastened his own pair with a quickness that projected familiarity with the act.

"I think I'm developing nerves."

"You'll be okay. I won't let you fall."

Good news since she had little faith in her own ability to keep her from falling flat on her behind. Toni twisted her mouth so she could talk out of the side of it, lowered her voice into a threatening one. "You better be good, brother."

Blake stood, his eyes lit with a mischievous shine. "You can trust me."

"Why do I sense a double meaning in your words?" Toni cautiously stood and clutched the hand he held out.

"Okay, loosen up. Relax. Get your balance. Just stand there a minute and get the feel of the blades.

Toni straightened, loosened her hold and took a deep breath. She hoped she didn't end up being the laughing stock of the evening. A broken neck was all she needed.

A teenaged skater swept by, and the swishing air pulled at her. She leaned into it, measuring the delicate balance she needed to keep her feet under her.

"Feel better?"

"I think so."

"Ready to try it?"

Toni heaved another breath. "I think so."

"Then let's let 'er rip."

They glided forward. At first Toni thought she would embarrass herself, but by the time they reached the middle of the pond, her confidence had climbed. This was fun. She loosened her grip a little more, although she was glad for Blake's steadying hands.

Half an hour later, they were back at their starting point.

"Ready for a break?" Blake made sure she was secure near the light post, then glided a little ways off, circling and twisting in fancy moves.

Toni watched him, admiring his graceful action, confidence in every move. He'd changed from an awkward waddling duck into an elegant swan. "I'd like to go at it a little longer. I'm just starting to feel confident."

"Ready to venture out on your own?" Blake cast a glance up the path.

"I'll be fine. Go have fun."

He glided around her, making her dizzy with his suave maneuvers. "Are you sure? I don't mind skating with you."

They'd passed Britney—Stan's daughter—back a ways. Toni figured Blake was anxious to go say hi. He'd have more fun with people his own age, without her tagging along. After all, she'd done this for him. She called after him as he took off. "Meet me back here in an hour."

He acknowledged her statement with a wave

and was off like a speed demon.

Toni skated another fifteen minutes, enjoying her solitude, nodding at those she passed, stopping—with a jerk—to speak with the few she knew.

Once she saw Blake and Britney in the distance. It looked like they were racing. She held her breath while the young, lithe figures glided out of view. Old, that's how she felt compared to their vitality. She allowed herself a grim smile. Had she figured on staying young forever like Peter Pan?

The weekend food stand was grilling, and the smell of pulled pork was appetizingly divine. The three-quarters of a taco she'd devoured for supper seemed a lifetime away. She looked down at the skates on her feet. Could she make it over to the food court by herself?

If she could manage to get back to their starting point Blake might be there. No doubt, hungry again. Since it was Friday night, they'd treat themselves to a late night and stop at one of the food stands to refuel his energy. Maybe Stan would allow Britney to go with them.

Toby Gibson and his current girlfriend walked by. "Hey, Toni. How's it going?" They paused to talk. "Didn't know you could skate."

"I don't really." Toni came to an abrupt stop, laughing. "Hi, Ginger."

The girl nodded at her.

"Blake is teaching me."

Toby looked around. "Where is he?"

"I sent him off to join Britney Robinson. He needed to be with someone his own age." She sat down and started to unlace her blades.

"Here, let me help." Toby dropped to one knee.

Toni's face warmed. At one time, Toby had shown interest in her. But that'd been eons ago. He'd gone through a lot of girlfriends since then. She hoped he didn't entertain any feelings like that now.

Ginger stared at Toby, an unhappy expression radiating out of her hazel eyes. Was she jealous? Well, she had nothing to worry about. She loved Toby like a brother and could never consider him as anything else.

Besides, there was the possibility of Perrin.

As soon as Toby finished, she said good-by and watched them walk away arm in arm, without seeing them. In her mind, she saw a pair of blue-green eyes and a handsome head of chestnut wavy hair. How much more fun tonight would have been if he'd been here.

But he wasn't.

Chapter Twenty-three

Ten o'clock. Not too late, maybe, to give Toni a call. He was past due to talk with Blake anyway.

He let the phone ring twelve times before setting the receiver back in its cradle. Perrin frowned. Where could she be?

~*~

Toni turned the skates into the rental booth, walked toward the food court, hoping to see Blake and Britney. She hadn't walked fifty feet when Toby appeared around a bend running at full tilt.

"What's wrong?" she asked as Toby stopped in front of her.

"It's Blake."

Toni ran with Toby keeping pace beside her. On the other side of the food court, a crowd had gathered, but two park officers kept them away. Toni, with Toby's help, pushed through.

"What's wrong, Britney? Where's Blake?" The panic that pressed against her insides pitched her voice higher than should have been.

Britney's hand covered her mouth, huge tears pooled in her eyes.

"I don't know. Two people came up to us and grabbed him. He tried to get loose, but they were too strong for him." The girl bit her lip. "I couldn't do anything."

"It's okay, honey." Toni slipped an arm around the shaking girl. "Did you give the detectives descriptions?"

Britney's head bobbed.

"Will you call Perrin?" Toni looked up at Toby. "His number is 555-0908."

He nodded and patted her shoulder.

"Toby?" she whispered. "Prayers please."

She was going to need all the prayers she could get when she faced Perrin's accusing eyes.

~*~

Toni sat hunched, her knees drawn up to her chin, her arms wrapped around them, her head laid upon them. The last time she'd looked it'd been 2:30 a.m.

Caro had come by and stayed two hours. Starli had stopped after closing hours for her restaurant. She'd brought hot soup and coffee, but Toni's stomach had churned at the thought of eating. She'd sent them both home ten minutes ago.

She remembered when Perrin had given her the permission papers for Blake. "Just in case." They'd laughed. As if something would ever happen.

Right.

She prayed now. Prayed for Blake. Perrin. Britney. Herself. Anyone to keep her mind off what had happened. Tears stung her eyes, and she brushed them away. "Why, God? Every time I think Perrin is softening up, something else happens that hardens his heart."

Loud voices interrupted her musings, and she looked up and saw a group of people headed her way. There were too many policemen at first, and then...she saw him. Blake.

Before her feet could touch the floor, he was moving toward her, looking a little bit relieved and a whole lot of embarrassed. The policemen followed like blue dragon tails.

"Blake, are you all right? What happened?" Throwing her arms around him, she hugged him tightly. She didn't care how embarrassed *he* was.

He pulled back. "I'm fine, Toni. Quit fussing."

"I know." Her throat clogged.

"I knew what I was doing." He was patting her back, comforting *her*.

"What do you mean, dear?"

The boy shrugged. "It wasn't a big deal. These two guys grabbed me, and I fought them trying to get loose. But as soon as we got out of the park, they let me go and explained they just wanted to talk a few minutes."

What? Toni's gaze met Detective Eddie's serious eyes. "You walked all the way here? Didn't you have your cell?"

"Yeah, and I left my phone at home."

"What did they want to talk about?" The policeman spoke in a gentle tone.

Another shrug. "I don't know. We didn't really talk about anything important. After about twenty minutes, they took off."

Didn't make sense. Were they trying to make a scene? Was it just kid-pranks, picking on a younger kid?

"Do you think it was adults, Blake?"

"Nah." He shook his head then amended, "Maybe. One was small. About my size. The other taller."

"Were they making fun of you? Maybe laughing or being rude?"

"Nope. They didn't say much until we stopped, then we chatted about school and sports and stuff."

"Can you describe them?"

It was the detective again.

"Couldn't see their faces. Hats on and scarves wrapped around their faces. Only their eyes." Blake grinned. "One had blue eyes-very blue, and the other kind of a hazel."

"And that's all they did or said?" Incredulity rang in the deputy's voice.

"Mostly. They patted my shoulder like I was a little kid and told me I could go on back to Toni."

"They said *that*? They named me out?"

He nodded.

Toni plopped back onto the bench. This wasn't a kidnapping. It was harassment for her. They hadn't wanted to harm Blake; only scare her.

But why?

This wasn't funny. As long as it had involved her, she lived with it. But people she loved?

~*~

Blake leaned against the back of his barstool, while Toni beat eggs in a blue ceramic bowl.

The meat was browning on the back burner of her stove. Toni pointed a fork at Blake. "You get those peppers and green onions chopped, my lad, or no supper for you."

Blake whined back at her. "Why do I have to do this? I was kidnapped yesterday."

Toni sniffed and raised her brows. "You know why. I did your turn at dishes two nights ago and this morning too. The ones that didn't get done last night because we went to the park. Fair division of labor around here. Your words. Remember?"

"I hate this job." Blake grumbled and swiped at the tears running down his cheeks. He sighed. "Is this lasagna worth it? I don't want salad anyway. Why don't we call out for pizza?"

Toni allowed a mock-horror expression to twist her face. "Pizza? Pizza? You haven't tasted anything until you've tried my lasagna. You'll be begging to cut onions."

"Yeah, right."

"I wonder if I could have some lasagna?"

Toni's stomach tightened, and she whirled, shock spreading through her whole body. She caught a glimpse of Blake's equally surprised eyes, his mouth open, for once too surprised to talk.

Perrin leaned against the doorway, his big frame casual and relaxed. Unlike the last time she'd seen him, tonight he was dressed as if he expected a casual night at home. His blue open-necked golfer's shirt and tan khakis were creased and spotless. His brown boat shoes were shined. His curls had been tamed, although one or two had begun their spiraling curves. The searching blue-green eyes behind the gold frames looked from Toni to Blake.

Charms ambled over to the man and began her sleek winding methods around his legs. Perrin unfolded his crossed legs and bent to stroke the cat, then picked her up and peered down at her. "I think, my lady, that you've stolen their tongues."

He dropped the cat and smiled. "Well? Are you two going to tell me how much you've missed me?"

"Dad." Blake dropped his knife and scrambled toward him. "How long can you stay?"

"How about forever?"

Blake's answer was a shout.

Toni didn't move. Her feet had frozen in the warm kitchen. She knew she should welcome him. Tell him she was glad he'd come home for a visit.

Perrin hugged his son, then kept an arm slung about his son's shoulder as Blake rambled on about school.

A sensation of happiness rippled through her. Hopefully, the grin on her lips didn't look as silly as it felt.

She should ask why he was home. She should check her lasagna noodles again. She should ask him if he wanted a drink. She should...

Perrin looked over at her. "What can I do? I'm hungry. How long before the lasagna is done?" His eyes twinkled at her.

"Would you like a drink? There's tea and fresh lemonade. The sauce is ready." She looked over at Blake. "Are those onions chopped?"

"Ah, do I have to finish them?"

"Here, let me do that." Perrin reached for the knife.

"Since there's nothing for me to do, I'm going to call Sid to come over." Blake grinned at Toni. "See ya."

But he was back in seconds.

"I forgot to tell you, Toni." The boy trotted up to her and breathed over her neck. "I knew there was something familiar about my two kidnappers."

"You know who they are?"

"No. I just remembered why one of them seemed familiar."

"Well, are you going to tell me?" Toni teased although she thought her heart might stop from sheer suspense.

"Her smell."

Her? Smell?

"You're saying a woman kidnapped you? What did she smell like?"

"I didn't realize it was a woman until I remembered the smell." The boy crinkled up his nose in disgust. "Strong. Kind of sickening and—what's that flower-vine in the spring with the purple blossoms?"

"Wisteria."

"Yep, and I smelled it before. Remember when you and dad and I went for ice cream after eating at Apple Blossoms when dad wanted to—"

"Blake, go on with your memory."

Perrin did look a bit flushed. Had that interruption been to stop what the boy was about to say?

"I kept smelling it then. Every time people would pass me, I smelled it."

"*Everyone?*" That made no sense.

"No, just when—"

It was Toni's turn to interrupt this time. "I think I know who you mean. Thank you, Blake. That's a big help."

Blake turned away, but Toni stopped him. "Wait. Blake remember when you mentioned seeing someone several times but didn't know who they were? Did you think then or now that they might be following—you?"

"I dunno. I mean, I kept seeing him, and guess I wondered why every time I was with you, he showed up."

"It was a man?"

"Yeah. Kinda tall, a bit scruffy, but fashionably so, I think." He rubbed his nose. "I probably wouldn't have noticed him, but every time I stared at him, he would turn away or move like he was some kind of PI. Sorta stupid."

"Dirty blond hair?"

"Yep. That was him."

Kevin Meyers.

As Blake clomped down the hall, Perrin began chopping the vegetable with a vengeance. "What did you mean just then? Who was this guy? Was he following Blake? And do you know now who's sending those cards?"

"It was Kevin Meyers, and he was following me." Toni hesitated. "I think I know who's behind the notes. It's kind of shaping up in my head. Pieces are starting to tie together. At first I couldn't think anyone here in Appleton would do the things that were happening, but then those pieces started meaning more."

"And now, you have some ideas that seem possible."

"I'm afraid so." Toni checked her noodles, turned the fire down, and sat down opposite Perrin. "Why are you home? Are you finished promoting your book?"

He gave her a cheeky grin. "For this weekend."

When she questioned him with her eyes, he elaborated. "Actually, I told them, I wouldn't work like that anymore. They could either have the weekends or the week. Their choice, but I had to have one or the other free every week. My family needed me."

"He's doing fine," Toni clasped her hands together, "but I know he misses you."

"And I miss him." Perrin's smile vanished. He tossed down the knife and wiped his hands. Then he reached across the table and took one of hers. "And I missed you."

"I missed you too." Toni whispered the words, but she knew Perrin heard.

He lifted her hand, inspected it and sent her a sly grin. "You've been working on a car while I've been gone, haven't you?"

She wrinkled her nose at him, but he gave her no time to answer. With a final squeeze of her hand, he let go, and resumed his chopping. "How's this?"

"Good. So you have the whole weekend off."

"The whole weekend till late Sunday night. And I've made a decision." He drew in a long breath. "I can't say I feel any different yet, but I'm going to give church a shot."

Toni heard the words but couldn't believe them. "What did you say?"

"I came home to go to church with you..."

"You're not kidding?" No, he wouldn't do that.

"Of course not." Perrin stood and took the scraps of vegetables over to the sink to dump them down the disposal. Then he rinsed the board and knife, placed them in the drainer, washed his hands, and sat down. "I have to be honest. Mostly, right now, I'm going for you. But I think, I'm almost sure, there's a stirring of interest to find out if the God you serve is real and can be for me."

His eyes were earnest as he talked. "Toni, when you called about Blake's kidnapping, I almost reverted to my old ways. I started to blame you. You were careless, you had been too lax with him, and too permissive."

He stood and walked to her window. "Something stopped me." He turned his head and stared at her in wonder. "It was your face. All I could see was your beautiful, heart-shaped face. The honesty in your eyes. You, so full of life and love and sweetness for a couple of characters new to Appleton."

He pulled the barstool closer to her and sat. "There was no way that anything could be your fault. You've cared too deeply for this renegade family. You've shown God's love for us. You've shown us the way to God."

"I just tried to be a friend to a cranky neighbor."

"That's true. Blake's desire for church ate at me. Gnawed at me that for all my love for the boy, I'd neglected something vitally important."

Toni nodded her understanding just as her cell gave its particular ring for Roxie Polinsky.

Chapter Twenty-four

"Some lawyer called wanting you to call back." Roxie's indignant tone clued Toni in that she wasn't a happy secretary. "I tried to tell him it was the weekend, and you'd call him Monday, but he'd have none of it. Tonight, or barring that, first thing in the morning. Sorry, Toni."

Toni soothed her distraught secretary and turned back to Perrin as she laid her cell on the countertop. "Some lawyer wants to talk with me."

"Problems?" Perrin's gaze questioned her.

"Not that I know of. Still, it's a little puzzling. Do you think it's too late to give him a call? Roxie indicated he wanted me to call tonight."

"Go ahead."

There was no way she could wait. If it was bad news she wanted to hear it tonight and get it over with. Her finger pressed the keys, and seconds later, she was identifying herself.

"It's about time, Miss DeLuca. Thought I'd never hear your voice." His gruff voice sent goose bumps up her arm. "Be at my office in Charleston at ten in the morning. Don't be late."

What? Toni pulled the cell from her ear and glared at it. What kind of attorney demanded and expected to be obeyed?

"I guess I'm to see him in the morning." Toni

rubbed her forehead, dread sending a nervous shiver through her body. "I can't imagine why, but my imagination wants to create a bunch of scary scenarios of could-be's."

"I'll be glad to go with you."

She couldn't ask that of him, but oh, how she'd love it. "I can't ask—"

Perrin's hand covered hers. "I wouldn't have volunteered, if I hadn't been willing."

Her heart melted a bit more.

~*~

Toni stared up at the tall brick building. The unassuming sign announced the occupants: Attorneys at Law, John, Richard, and Leslie Mason.

Checking the floor number, Toni, with Perrin beside her, stepped into the elevator. The ride was smooth, with nary a bump, and the doors slid open, as if they'd been liberally doused in some kind of lubricant, to an opulent room.

A stylish woman sat at a desk and looked up. "May I help you?"

"Antonietta DeLuca and Perrin Douglas to see John Mason."

"He's expecting you. Right this way, please."

Toni followed the blond down the hall where she swung open the door and announced their names.

A gruff voice beckoned them to enter, and Toni stepped into the room and spotted Detective Eddie standing close to the lawyer's desk.

Toni abruptly stopped walking. "Eddie, what are you doing—?"

The lawyer stood and moved toward them to

shake their hands. "Your great grandparents are Gerald and Clarissa Jones?"

"Yes. At least I know that was his name. I've never known hers." Toni stared straight into the man's eyes. He didn't look like a shark, but was he?

"I see. With their recent death, there's a matter of business concerning their properties."

"I didn't know them or they me. Isn't there other family who'd be better equipped to handle this? I can't see why it should concern me."

"You've got that right," A voice snapped behind her.

She knew that voice. Toni whirled. "Rita Mae? Why are you here? I'm totally confused."

"Why are *you* here?" Rita shot back. There was no welcome in Rita's eyes.

And at the opposite end of the room, two people turned to face her. A distinguished man with a beard and narrow eyes. Sal.

Sylvia Searles, her hand resting lightly on Sal's arm, frowned at Toni, even as she beckoned her son closer.

"What's going on, Arnie?" Better to ignore the bane-of-her-life-woman. Arnie, at least, had enough sense to respond reasonably.

But he didn't have time. John Mason interrupted. "Please, everyone, take a seat."

"I want to know now what is going on." Toni demanded, her temper surging. Was this some kind of trick? Another insult to herself in person instead of those stupid, *smelly* pink cards?

"I'll explain everything if you'll just have a

seat."

"Sir, you have five minutes to explain why you demanded I show up, before I'm out of here." Normally as soft spoken as her Italian heritage would allow her to be, she'd had enough. Enduring those sabotaged construction jobs and too many recent threats had pushed her to the limit.

Perrin's hand touched her back. Gently, he guided her to the long, dark table and seated her, his voice low and calm as he whispered. "Take a few minutes to hear what he says. He wouldn't have called you if it wasn't important."

"Thank you." The attorney seemed relieved although far from being rattled.

Was she suppose to say, 'You're welcome'? Well, she wouldn't. The longer she was in this room with a demanding lawyer she didn't know and this—this group of Appleton folks, the more frustrated she felt. "Tell me now why I was summoned here."

"There are complications."

Wasn't there always?

"If you'll give me a few minutes, I will explain, Miss DeLuca."

Perrin's big hand reached for hers under the table and gave it a light squeeze. *Keep calm,* it seemed to encourage.

She didn't want to. All she wanted was to walk out of here and forget she had grandparents and great grandparents who hadn't cared enough about her to keep in touch. Why would she be interested in anything they had to say after their death?

Another squeeze, and she gave in. She

nodded at the attorney.

He breathed a sigh of relief. "With the passing of Clarissa Jones, she left us as the executor of her will. For a long time, the will did not change. Then a year before her death, she called to make some changes. In the new will, there are requirements about who is to inherit."

"Inherit?" Toni interrupted. "I didn't realize this meeting had anything to do with an inheritance. I should be the last person included in this discussion."

"I agree. Why should Toni, who had nothing to do with them, be here?" Rita Mae lifted one shoulder in a shrug that said the statement defied her reasoning. "I mean, because her dad wanted to be as far away from them as possible, and wanted nothing to do with them, he changed his name."

"That's not true." Toni was horrified at the accusation.

"How would you know? Have you seen your birth certificate? Who was your real, birth father? Do you know?" Rita Mae's words slashed at her.

Suddenly, Toni was determined to stay. She'd not have a—a tart like *her* tell her when to leave.

"For that matter, why is *she* here?" She cocked her head in Rita Mae's direction. "Did she work for them?"

Rita Mae's splutter was loud.

"She has a birth certificate, all right." The attorney's quiet interjected remark sent a ripple of emotion around the room.

"She does? I couldn't find—"

"It exists all the same." Mr. Mason nodded. "Took us almost too long to discover Gerald Jones had bribed the county clerks to turn over any birth certificate information to him. That's one reason why we couldn't find you until now, Miss DeLuca."

Rita Mae sat forward. "And I'm demanding proof of this. How are we to know you aren't in on a scheme to get some of the money?"

"That makes no sense, Rita Mae," Perrin offered. "I'm sure, if the Jones had money, they also had accountants. I seriously doubt this law firm handled that side of their affairs."

"That's so, Mr. Douglas," the attorney agreed. "And we do have signatures and proof of the new will. Miss DeLuca, you might as well go ahead with your questions. I see we'll not be able to finish until you and Miss Simpson iron this out."

"It took me awhile to figure out who was behind my recent problems."

The woman slid a sly glance at first the lawyer then at Perrin. "What are you talking about?"

"The pink cards. The phone calls. The old birth certificate."

"I didn't—"

"I know you did."

Rita's face had aged in just the few seconds she'd faced her. Toni knew the woman had to be close to her father's age, but Rita had always looked and acted younger. Her friends had been years younger. She'd been giddy and loud. Pushy and flirty. People either loved her or hated her. They either followed her or avoided her.

Yet she was smart. She'd started the café and worked hard to make it a success. She had talent leading their Christmas and Easter dramas the church produced.

"Well, it's all your fault, you know." Rita's eyes flashed at her, accusing and a little bit angry. "You kept your father and me from getting together."

It was news to her. "How did I accomplish that? Regardless of what you think, I do not know what you're talking about." If she repeated the denial enough, would Rita believe it?

"Are you saying, you don't remember your father dating me?"

"No, I don't."

"You can't remember what a spoiled brat you were?"

Maybe she had been spoiled, but any more than other children? Had she wanted her father's total attention so much he'd foregone having a relationship with a woman? She'd have to admit she'd never cared much for Rita Mae. Even as a child she'd thought she was fake. Had she been scared Rita would take away the only parent she had?

"All this has nothing to do with you sending me threats." Toni straightened.

Rita Mae smirked but refused to answer.

"What you did to me was wrong. I can't believe you would do that for some childish action from long ago."

"You? You? Is that all you can think about? What about me? Because of a little girl who couldn't share, I had to give up a chance of lifetime happiness." Rita's chest heaved. Her hair stood on end, mussed from hands that wouldn't leave it alone.

And Toni remembered the pictures in her box. The frowning, messy-haired, almost-a-woman who glared down at...her. Even then, Rita Mae had harbored a grudge against a child.

"I vowed then, someday I'd make you hurt like I hurt the night your father said it'd be better if we didn't see each other again."

The lawyer sat forward and finally spoke. "Miss Simpson, if Miss DeLuca's accusations are correct, you could be in serious trouble for those threats."

"Nonsense." Rita Mae waved away his warning.

Toni's gaze fastened on that waving hand. That scratch...

And her memory clicked. Her bedroom. The intruder. Toni latching on with her fingernails and digging in.

"No one can prove I damaged her property—"

"How do you know Toni's property was damaged?" Perrin shot the question out so quickly Toni blinked.

"It's all over town—"

"No, it's not. Only a handful of people knew about the sabotaging."

Wow. Perrin was quick on the draw. His scholarly mind stood him in good stead today.

"A friend saw you with those atrocious scented pink cards. I've got someone who recognized your perfume the night you and your accomplice kidnapped Blake Douglas. And I think with a little squeezing, Detective

Eddie can get your partner in crime talking." Toni tossed out the final words of condemnation on the vindictive woman.

Rita Mae jumped to her feet and flapped a hand at them. "All that means little. So what if I use pink cards? How many women do you suppose use the same type of perfume I do, just here in West Virginia? And I've never seen Kevin Myers before in my life."

Toni laughed, and even stern Mr. Jones hid a chuckle behind his hand, then raised it, probably hoping to stop World War Three.

"Miss Rita Mae," Detective Eddy also stood to his feet and blocked her way in her hurried retreat to the door. "I want to have a serious talk with you. Don't you be leaving Appleton till that happens. You're in serious trouble, ma'am."

Rita Mae said nothing, only stared at the detective, then flounced her way out the door, tossing back the threat. "I'm not done. I will fight this. You'll be hearing from me, Mr. Mason."

"Let's get back to the business at hand. You can sort out these accusations later." Obviously, Mr. Mason wasn't the least concerned at the threat Rita Mae had shot at him. So much for knowing the law.

"I'm not quite finished, Sir."

The long suffering attorney glared at Toni for a minute, growled under his breath, then nodded. "Go ahead then. Get it done with."

Toni shifted in her chair to stare at Sylvia. "And you. I'm tired of you trying to push Arnie and me together. I know you want the best for him, but it's not going to happen between

Arnie and me. Arnie's a smart and handsome guy. Let him—and me—alone. He can make his own choices and doesn't need his mother for that."

Sylvia's face flamed hot red. "Really, Toni? You are—"

"I've tried to be gentle before in refusing your not-so-subtle hints. But when you go so far as to spread rumors that I'm sabotaging my own business to get the insurance money, then my patience has run out."

"I did no such thing."

"You did, and I know it. You are the only one who had knowledge—because you work at the office where I put in an insurance claim to cover my losses. You are the only one who had a reason to do that in trying to force Arnie and me together. And what is worse, you helped Rita Mae kidnap Blake Douglas, didn't you?"

"Mother, you didn't." Arnie's outraged voice over rode Sylvia's protests. "That's it. Toni's right. I've had enough of your interference."

Arnie strode to the door, but tossed back his last deference to his maternal parent. "I'll leave the car for you."

"See what you've done." Sylvia threw at Toni as she ran after her son.

Even as the weight lifted off of Toni, depression sucked at her. Had she been too hard on the two women? Not on Rita Mae, for sure. Sylvia? Perhaps.

The lawyer shuffled papers then glanced at Sal. "Well, do you want to say anything before we move on?"

"Not at all. Please." He gave the attorney a slight bow.

"Then I'll proceed. Here's the story. I will run through the facts quickly. If you want more detail, you can ask questions later."

When no one spoke, he went on. "Gerald and Clarissa had only one son, which was your grandfather, Miss DeLuca. Sander Jones was his name. Their daughter was Sandra, named after her father. She died young, leaving one daughter, which was you."

Mr. Mason looked at her, and Toni nodded agreement. So far, it all made sense.

"Right after your father took custody of you, your grandparents were killed in an accident. That left only your great grandparents. Their will was simple. Half was to go to any relatives from your great grandmother's side, as Gerald had no family living. The other half was to be distributed among the remaining staff employed by them and a few charities they'd supported through the years."

She leaned forward. "Who was on Clarissa Jones' side of the family? And what if there was more than one?"

"There are several, but none as close as you are. If you weren't in the picture, all of them would split the half."

"Okay. So what happened?"

"I'm getting there. The reason there was supposedly no remaining members on Gerald's side was..."

"Yes?"

"Your father and Clarissa fought. She vowed to disinherit you and forbade your great grandfather to leave anything to you, should she die first. She had already refused to allow Sandra to name Danny DeLuca as your father, so that space on the certificate was left blank."

"But I thought you said—"

"I did. But, unknown to anyone else, Gerald Jones had encouraged Sandra and her parents to have a second, and correct, birth certificate made, naming Danny DeLuca as the father and giving you his last name. He placed it in a deposit box with other papers he kept secret from his wife. We were able to ascertain information about it only because of a trusted man servant who passed the information on to us for a meager reward."

"I see." To think that a grandmother could hate so much...

"Gerald Jones did pass away first. That left Clarissa. But in her final days, she had a change of heart."

"In her final hours, she called her most trusted employees and myself, and her physician—who has provided us with a signed and stamped document that Clarissa was of clear mind, even to her dying hour—to witness the new will. Everything was handled legally, fairly and clearly."

A weight settled over Toni, and with dread, she questioned, "And how was it changed, Mr. Mason?"

"You see, after her death, we began searching for any and all relatives who could have a claim. After an extensive and exhaustive search, the only one we could find was Miss Simpson."

So she was an employee. But he'd just said he was searching for relatives. That meant Rita Mae—and herself—no, it couldn't be. Related all these years and not know it? But it seemed she hadn't known much about any of her distant family.

"When did my great grandmother pass away? Why hasn't the money already been distributed?"

"Because, as I mentioned before there were complications."

"And they are?" The sooner this was over, the sooner she and Perrin could leave.

He'd been awfully quiet. Toni glanced at her friend. His face was serious; his attitude interested.

At least she had one friend in this room.

"There was a time-hold before the will could be executed."

"Meaning?"

"We were to have one year to search for any remaining relatives. Clarissa knew of at least one niece, which was Miss Simpson. The tie was a loose one because Miss Simpson was Clarissa's estranged sister's daughter."

Well...at least she and Rita Mae weren't *close* relatives. For some reason, that thought tickled her, and she gave a choked up chuckle. She caught Perrin's quick glance at her and was sure his lips widened in agreement. Perhaps he'd read her mind?

"Then," Toni swiveled a little to look at Sal, "why are you here, Sal?"

The man hmmmed and started to speak, but Mr. Mason beat him to it.

"He is even more loosely tied with the situation, although he's tried to make a strong case of it. Six weeks ago, he put in his claim because he is Clarissa's half-brother's son."

No one said a word.

"What?" This was too much to take in. Toni felt the blood draining from her head, the dizziness swirling inside her brain.

"Here. Drink this, Toni." Perrin set a glass of water in her hands.

Toni sipped at the water and felt the dizziness subsiding. Two long breaths, and then she spoke. "So why did you propose to me?"

Sal smiled. "Why not? That would have been double insurance the money would come to me."

"You—" Perrin started to speak, half rising, but Toni stopped him.

"It's okay. I want to hear him."

"I knew my cousin. Knew what she is capable of. She was always a selfish child, and that is what brought me here to your beautiful town. When she tried to drag me into her scheme, I realized I would have to do my best to stop her."

How touching. Did he really think she was that gullible? "So you were so concerned for my welfare you put in a claim? Was that your plan?"

"I see you don't understand fully my thoughts, my dear." Sal stood and sauntered across the room. "It would have been a good plan, had it succeeded."

He thrust open the door and looked back at her. "Rest assured, Antonietta, that I would have been honored to have you as my wife."

She could just imagine. The audacity of people. "Can you believe him?"

And then she was laughing. Perrin's mouth crooked up. Even Mr. Mason sent her a grin.

"Are you okay?"

"I'm fine."

"Not too disappointed?"

Toni scorned her friend with a look. "At Sal's false proposal? You have to ask?"

"So where does that leave Toni, Mr. Mason?" Perrin asked.

"Right where she should be. As the legal claimant of property that, in due process, will go to her."

"You mentioned a time hold. Is that still ongoing? When is this time limit up?"

The older man looked at her over her glasses. "Tonight, at midnight."

"That's cutting it close."

"Yes, but until yesterday, we had no clue you even existed."

"How can that be? I mean, daddy didn't change his name."

John Mason smiled. "But he did, my dear. He certainly did."

Chapter Twenty-five

"**W**hy do you suppose Daddy changed our surname?"

Arm and arm, Toni and Perrin walked down the street, the air crisp, and the heavy, snow-laden clouds hanging low over Appleton. Her cheeks felt as cold as an iced drink, but her hands were warm and snug, tucked within Perrin's arm. She wanted to rub her cheek against his strong shoulder, but refrained. His answer was important to her.

"We could speculate all night, and might never guess the real reason."

"But I want to know what you think."

"Then, my princess, you shall hear it." He grinned at her. "Mr. Mason said your father and great grandmother had a serious fight. I'm thinking it was so disagreeable that after your father won custody of you, he didn't want you or himself to be bothered or have contact with them. You with me so far?"

"Yes."

"I got the impression, Clarissa Jones was quite the matriarch in that family. If any of that money came from her side of the family, she probably kept a tight rein on it. Thus when Danny DeLuca, beat her at her own game—in gaining custody of you, she vowed to make you both suffer, not realizing, or maybe not caring, that some people don't consider money as the most important object in their lives."

"Are you saying, after their fight, Daddy changed his name to keep them from finding us, and Clarissa—I can't call her great grandmother!—thought she'd make him suffer by cutting me out of her will?"

"Sounds about how I figured it. Of course, there's no proof, and you'll probably never know for sure. But does it matter?" Perrin peered down at her.

Toni walked on without saying anything for a minute or so, thinking about what he'd said. "No. No, it doesn't. I'm sad at the sadness in all this, but I can't change it."

"No, you can't." Perrin slipped an arm around her, pulling her closer. "What are you doing about Rita Mae?"

"Hmmm. That's a different story. She's threatening to appeal on the grounds that I'm adopted, if she doesn't get some of the money."

"But you're not."

"Yeah, I know that, and you know that, but obviously she thinks because my surname *now* wasn't on the first—the original—birth certificate, Daddy adopted me. Crazy, isn't it? Mr. Mason says with all that she's done to threaten and sabotage my business, it's unlikely she can hire a legitimate lawyer who can make her protests stick. Still..."

"Are you afraid?"

"Not about losing the money, no. I don't even want it." Toni gave a half-embarrassed laugh. "I feel guilty about ruining her chance at happiness with my dad. I can't remember doing it, but I can remember not liking her when I was a child."

"That is certainly not your fault."

"I realize that, but what would it hurt to share a little? I don't need the money, and if it would help her to forgive and forget, it would be worth sharing with her."

"Toni DeLuca, you're more wonderful every time I see you."

"I doubt that, but I love hearing you say it."

"What does old man Mason say about that?"

"He frowned at me, argued a little, but said he'd check out the reasonability of it. He'll come around."

A flake of snow fluttered to earth and landed on Perrin's dark hair. Another one floated downward, and then the flakes came faster until they both were covered in a white blanket.

"Shall we hurry home before we get snowed in, here in town?"

"Don't worry about that. I'll see that you get home safely. Blake's with Sid and his parents at Apple Blossoms right now. Let's go there."

With an enthusiastic nod, Toni agreed. "Sounds perfect."

Perrin laughed and guided her toward the restaurant. "Time for some hot chocolate."

~*~

Toni and Perrin sipped their chocolate, and she laughed. "You look kind of grand with a mustache."

"You don't look bad yourself," Perrin bent forward to wipe her upper lip with a napkin.

With a quiet sigh, Toni sat back.

"Are you sad, my princess?" His eyes implored assurance from her.

"Not at all. My insides are about to explode

with happiness at having you and Blake in my life."

"Do you remember all those questions I wanted to ask you when I was still uncertain about hiring DeLuca Construction?" Perrin turned his cup in a slow circle. "Well, I've changed my questions to just one: Would you like to take on the job permanently?"

"What job?"

"Caring for Blake—"

"You want to give Blake to me? Perrin, how could you? It would break his heart."

He lifted his gaze then and stared straight into her eyes. "Not if you took me on too as part of the job."

What was he saying?

"I don't understand. I'll always be your friend. You should know that." Would her heart quit beating from anticipation?

"I want more than that. I'm asking you to marry me."

Toni's breath left her body in a whoosh. She stared at him, seeing his eyes, earnest and blue, and a little bit anxious, question her. He was serious. He'd just asked her to...

"You're serious?" she whispered the words, as if they were a secret.

"I wouldn't tease about something like that. I think too much of you."

"But, you haven't said anything about..." She was afraid to say the word. What if she was wrong, and he just wanted a glorified babysitter while he was gallivanting all over the country getting famous?

"About love?" Perrin stood and drew her to her feet, obviously forgetting where they were.

He turned her to face him and took both her hands. "Toni DeLuca, will you marry me and walk by my side for the rest of our days?"

Not only was she having heart problems, her hearing must be getting bad.

He tilted his head. "You must remember. I can be an awfully selfish person sometimes."

"Oh, Perrin."

"Is that a yes or no?"

"Yes. It's a yes."

Perrin drew her close, and Toni laid her head against his chest, his strong arms surrounding her. She'd never felt so loved and protected. She, who had always been strong.

She could get use to the feeling.

A snicker filtered through to her, and she looked up.

Half the patrons in the room were clapping, some cheering, and Blake, with Sid behind him, peered at them, a wide grin on his face. "Whoops. Did you pop the question, Dad?"

Then slapping hands, the boys turned and pounded back to their table with Sid's parents.

"Did you tell him you were asking me to...?"

"Marry me?" Perrin finished her question. "Yes, I did. I wanted to make sure he had no objections. I knew he wouldn't, but if he would have, I would have read him the riot act."

"I see."

"Come back here for a minute, in my arms."

Perrin's whispering voice fanned the hair on her cheek.

She started to pull back, but he held her tight and tugged on her hand. "Let's walk."

She nodded, and they slipped into their coats and out the door.

The snow had covered the ground, and their boots made soft squishy sounds as they walked. The evening Christmas lights colored the snow that lay on the house roofs and ledges as they strolled down the sidewalk. The snowman beside the town gazebo gave them, as they passed, a cocky grin with his black coal-mouth.

Christmas was coming to Appleton.

Perrin was whispering again. This time into her ear. His breath was warm, his words music to her ears.

"I love you more than I thought I could love anyone." He lifted her hand, his gaze on her face, and brushed her fingertips with his lips.

Toni closed her eyes for just a second. Now *that* was how a man should kiss a woman's hand. The warmth expanded inside her as she mentally scribbled one more thing to her list of items she loved about Appleton, West Virginia.

The End

Other Books by Carole Brown

Denton and Alex Davies Mysteries:
Hog Insane
Bat Crazy

Spies of World War II
With Music In Their Hearts
A Flute in the Willows
Sing Until You Die

The Appleton WV Mysteries
Sabotaged Christmas
Knight in Shining Apron
Undiscovered Treasures
Toby's Troubles

Troubles in the West
Caleb's Destiny

Women's Fiction:
The Redemption of Caralynne Haymen

Misc
West Virginia Scrapbook
Christmas Angels (WW II short story in the Anthology *From the Lake to the River)*

Turn the page for a sneak peek at Book Two in the Appleton Romantic Mysteries. Enjoy the first chapter of *Knight in Shining Apron*

Carole Brown

An Appleton, WV Romantic Mystery

She can't run away
from her past. Will the
new chef help or hurt?

Apple Blossoms
Restaurant

Knight in
Shining Apron

Chapter One

Joel Peterman-Blair stepped further into the kitchen and leaned against a counter, his gaze fastened on the red-haired guy who wielded the large knife like he'd had plenty of practice.

The man's gaze lifted as if just aware that someone different had entered his domain.

Joel moved forward. "Hi. Uncle Lawrence—Manny sent for me. Wouldn't know where he is, would you?"

Suspicion, then disdain flickered in the brown eyes. With a frown, the man pointed the blade. "The new helper, are you? Last one we had just walked out. You're kind of old for the position."

Abashed at the man's bluntness, Joel stiffened. Old? Who did the bloke think he was?

Joel started to speak, but the man plowed on. "But if Manny wants you, Starli must have agreed. Who am I to complain?"

The knife flashed in the sunlight streaming through the huge windowpane over the sink. "Over there. Start on those pans. And you're too dressed up. Tomorrow, come without the tie."

Joel winked at the girl cutting vegetables at a large table. The man had mistaken him for a hired helper. Not half. A joke on Manny when

3

he found him doing dishes.

A monstrous apron hung on a peg beside the door. Joel tied it around his waist and rolled his sleeves above his elbows. When he turned on the taps, the hot water gushed into the sink. He poured a lavish supply of soap into the spray and dug in.

When was the last time he'd washed a pan? He couldn't remember. He wouldn't want his lady friends to see him, but...his whistle matched his washing pace.

Behind him the swinging door whooshed open, but he paid it no mind.

Joel eyed his progress. He'd made a serious dent in the pile of pans. One more, and he'd have the bunch done.

"Who *is* this?" A surprised female voice slashed through the quiet kitchen.

"It's the new guy Manny sent to help out. I thought you approved it, or I would have checked with you first."

Joel stacked the last pan and turned, water and suds dripping from his hands.

Luvly-jubbly. The most exquisite creature he'd ever seen waltzed across the room. Her white-blond hair, captured in a ponytail, bobbed, her green eyes blazed with distrust.

Giving him the once-over, was she? Oh, ho. Some acting was called for. He allowed himself another quick glance, nodded, then lowered his gaze. Might as well play along with the charade. His lips twitched. He could see Uncle Lawrence's face when he caught him doing the dishes. And playing this game. "Ma'am."

Tall and slender, she glided closer, her eyes

narrowed. "Who are you? You've got soap suds all over the floor."

Mirth swelled inside him, but he swallowed the temptation to laugh. He wouldn't have been surprised to see her stretch one long finger in haughty accusation at him, declaring, "Off with his head."

Joel glanced at the substantial puddle on the floor, then nodded toward the back door. "Through there. I thought all employ-hired help did that."

He risked staring into her eyes. She frowned, her perfect brows forming a V over the bridge of her straight nose. Joel hid another smile and couldn't resist teasing her.

"You must quit that frowning. You'll be old before your time."

"What do you know about frowns and women?" Her crisp voice reproved him. "You're a mess."

Joel looked down at himself, soaked from the dishwater. She was right. He was a mess. Beneath the apron, his red silk tie had bled onto his white shirt. Bully. What an impression he was making.

"Ma'am, you, on the other hand, look like the queen herself."

Her eyes sharpened.

"Only fairer. Much more so."

"Are you Irish? Your baloney is as thick as our autumn fog." Her tone slashed at him.

Something about her accent made him think she might be British. Or maybe Uncle Lawrence had rubbed off on her. He felt his lips stretch wider.

"Nay, my lady, but my great-granny was, bet

your bottom quid."

Her red lips curled and a snort emanated from her slender throat.

Very unladylike, but somehow impressive.

"Manny didn't hire you. I don't know what your game is, but it's up. Now. Get out."

He looked at her and the three employees standing behind her. The two women's sudden angry faces glared at him. Red-hair clutched his deadly knife. Joel raised both hands, but before he could speak the kitchen door swung open again.

"Joel? You're here? Why didn't you call me?" Uncle Lawrence's proper voice filled the room. He gripped the doorframe and gaped. "*What* are you doing?"

"The dishes." He gave a slight bow toward the sink, then crossed the room in long strides to gather his uncle in a wet hug. When at last he broke away, Joel laughed and pounded his uncle on the back.

A wide smile lit up the maitre de's features. He turned to the woman. "Miss Starli, my nephew, Sir Joel Peterman-Blair."

If a trumpet fanfare had blared out the announcement, it couldn't have been any more impressive.

"*Sir?* This man is your nephew?"

Joel bowed slightly, amused at her shocked tone. "At your service, ma'am."

"Stop calling me ma'am." She snapped.

"Yes, m..." Tongue in cheek, he spoke to his uncle, but his gaze remained fixed on the woman. "Mind telling me who this queen is?"

Manny glanced at Joel, but elaborated on

his explanation to Starli. "My *English* nephew, the chef I told you about."

"But 'sir'?"

"The Peterman-Blairs have ancestry, and Joel has the title. Hence, my relationship with the scoundrel." Manny's eyes twinkled.

"I see." She eyed Joel with skepticism. "Can he cook?"

"Can I? Ma'am—excuse me—you haven't eaten until you've tasted my scones." Joel swaggered a little. He turned to his uncle. "And who is the lovely lady, Uncle Lawrence?"

"Miss Starli Cameron. She owns Apple Blossoms and will be your employer."

Had he bitten into an unripe persimmon? His lips wanted to purse into a sour moue. "I see."

As if just aware that her employees were standing defensively about her, Miss Starli sighed. "It's okay, Louis. This...guy is Manny's nephew. Regardless of how he entered the restaurant."

She turned to Joel. "This is Louis Dupree, the assistant chef, and the kitchen help, Camille and Juanita."

Joel turned to the women and bowed slightly. The younger girl erupted into giggles. The older one looked pleased and bobbed her head. Only then did he switch his gaze to Louis, the red-haired man. There was no friendliness on his face. Mistrust and a bit of anger. Joel hesitated, knowing full well a little humbleness would go a long way to making friends with this man. "I'm depending on your help, friend."

Louis made no answer, only inclined his

head, his eyes sharp, dark, and watchful.

So much for humble pie.

Joel debated on whether to say more, but nodded, then followed his uncle and the owner out of the kitchen. Once in her office, she motioned for him to sit. Joel glanced at his uncle who edged toward the door.

"Manny, you're welcome to stay if you wish."

That sounded like a plea. Afraid of him, was she?

Again, Manny's gaze went to Joel even though he spoke to Starli. "I'll let you and Joel get acquainted."

Joel watched him leave and narrowed his eyes. What was his hurry? Something up his uncle's sleeve if he had to bet on it.

He turned back to the woman sitting on the opposite side of the desk. Her gaze, fastened on the doorway, darted to him, flicked away, then returned. She drew in a deep breath.

"Why are you here?"

Had Uncle Laurence not told her? "I thought you knew. Uncle Laurence said you needed a chef."

"Do you jump whenever Manny—your uncle—tells you of someone's need?"

"I'll let Uncle Laurence explain it to you." Joel crossed his legs and settled back into his chair.

"Manny told me you're an excellent chef."

"I am that."

She frowned at him. "Conceited, aren't you?"

"Convinced."

His snappy reply must not have done anything for Miss Starli. Her frown deepened.

Joel wanted to laugh.

"So Manny wants you to help us out for a time. Are you willing? What's your usual remuneration?"

Joel named a price.

"Are you worth it?"

"Bleeding right."

Starli's cheeks reddened. "If I hire you, I'll expect at least a five year agreement from you to stay on."

"Are we having a row already?" Joel's words were joking, but an undercurrent of daring flowed beneath his tone. "Let me check on the next flight back to England."

~*~

Manny's nephew sat back in his chair, one long leg crossed over the other. In spite of his ruined clothing, he exuded confidence. "I'm willing to take the job on one condition."

The man's blue eyes glowed with mirth and warmth. Did he think this meeting a joke?

Starli's mental hackles stood straight up. "What?"

"You have to get rid of the orange lights outside the restaurant. I can't work in a place that has orange lights decorating the outside."

"What?" Starli scowled at his smiling face.

"Just having a smattering of fun with you, Miss Starli. Haven't you ever heard the good book say laughter is good for the soul?" He peered at her as if he thought she never read the Bible.

"I read the Bible, Mr. Peterman-Blair. Excuse me, Sir Peterman-Blair."

"Joel will serve nicely. May I call you Starli?"

"No, you may not."

Now why had she refused? She never insisted any of her employees be so formal, but this man really got her. Time to take control of the situation.

"The five year agreement?"

"Bob's your uncle."

"What? Are you saying you won't stay five years?" Starli eyed him. He surely wasn't agreeing to her outrageous demand.

"Let's review our options in the morning. Shall we?"

"I insist you start in the morning." Might as well up the pressure a little.

"Corking. I'll just have a bit of a look around, if you don't mind. What are your hours?"

"Mine?"

"Sorry. The restaurant hours?"

"We open at four and close between ten and midnight. Depending. You'll be responsible for the evening meal and overseeing the kitchen staff."

Starli's gaze rested on the lock of golden blond hair that fell across his forehead. She jerked her gaze away. "Then we'll see you in the morning."

She heard him stride to the door and pause. His voice brought her gaze back to his face.

"You really should smile more often. You're a beautiful woman, and beautiful women should never frown. Takes fewer muscles to smile. Have a nice evening, Miss Starli." He snapped a jaunty salute at her.

Starli watched the door ease shut behind his tall form. For a long moment there was silence, then the sound of soft whistling drifted through the closed door.

What on earth had Manny gotten her into? If she'd ever seen trouble, this man and his casual air was it. He thought he could charm his way into what he wanted, did he?

Think again, Joel Peterman-Blair.

She just hoped she hadn't put her beloved restaurant at risk.

~*~

Early the next morning, Starli Cameron slashed off the last name on her list, the last possible candidate for hiring. In bold curves she wrote Joel Peterman-Blair at the bottom, then scratched the word sir at the front. Ripping the paper from the tablet, she crumpled it and tossed her pencil to the tabletop just as the phone rang.

Snatching up the receiver she struggled to control her voice. "Apple Blossoms. This is Starli Cameron.

"Starlie-e-e. Now fancy the stupid, undevoted wife being such a huge success." A pause. "Not quite fair, is it?"

Starli gripped the phone. *God, please, not again.* "What do you want? Why are you calling me?"

"Think you've got it made, don't you? While Ryan is decaying in the ground, his devoted wife is playing the high-rolling successful businesswoman to the tilt. You couldn't even give him a son, could you?"

A knife twisted in her heart. *Dear Lord, please help me.* "No. That's not—"

"Of course, it's true." The voice snapped, anger and threat resounding through it.

"I have to make a living." Desperation surged through her. She hated the whine in her voice.

"What about the hundred grand he left you? Remember that measly amount? Did you squander it? Hoard it?"

Starli's insides froze a little more. Was Roland Stratton, Ryan's twin brother, after the money? Too late. It'd all gone toward opening this restaurant.

She recognized the feelings raging through her. Anger, hurt, dismay, defeat. But she didn't want to address them. Didn't even want to acknowledge them.

"I went back to school and started this restaurant. That took money—"

"You're as stupid as Ryan always said. Too stupid to live." A coarse laugh grated through the receiver. "But you did, didn't you, Starlie-e-e? Ryan died, but you lived. Look down at that ugly finger of yours, Starlie-e-e."

Starli's gaze dropped to her left pinkie. The crooked one. The reminder. Fear thudded in her chest.

"Do you need another reminder?"

"No." The single word exploded from her throat.

The line went dead. He was gone. For now.

Award winning author Carole Brown loves to weave suspense and tough topics into her books, along with a touch of romance and whimsy.

She is always on the lookout for outstanding titles and catchy ideas.

Carole and Dan, her pastor husband, reside in SE Ohio and have ministered and counseled across the country. Together, they enjoy their grandsons, traveling, gardening, good food, the simple life, and did she mention their grandsons?

Carole loves to connect with her readers. You can find her at her blog:
Sunnebnkwrtr.blogspot.com/
And facebook:
www.facebook.com/CaroleBrown.author

If you enjoyed reading this book, let others know... and bless Carole Brown with an honest review.